PENGUIN METRO READS
ONE STRING ATTACHED

Pankaj Dubey is a bilingual novelist and film-maker. All his books, *What a Loser!*, *Ishqiyapa: To Hell with Love*, *Love Curry* and *Trending in Love*, published by Penguin Random House India, have been written by him in Hindi as well. He was a journalist with the BBC World Service in London. He was also selected for the prestigious Writers' Residency in the Seoul Art Space, Yeonhui, South Korea, among three novelists from Asia in 2016. He was awarded the Global Innoventure Award for Literature and Storytelling in the House of Lords, British Parliament, UK, in 2018. Two of his novels, *Trending in Love* and *Ishqiyapa*, are being adapted into web series. He can be followed on Twitter @carryonpd. To know more about him, visit https://en.wikipedia.org/wiki/Pankaj_Dubey.

One String Attached

PANKAJ DUBEY

Penguin
metro reads

An imprint of Penguin Random House

PENGUIN METRO READS

USA | Canada | UK | Ireland | Australia
New Zealand | India | South Africa | China

Penguin Metro Reads is part of the Penguin Random House group of companies
whose addresses can be found at global.penguinrandomhouse.com

Published by Penguin Random House India Pvt. Ltd
7th Floor, Infinity Tower C, DLF Cyber City,
Gurgaon 122 002, Haryana, India

Penguin
Random House
India

First published in Penguin Metro Reads by Penguin Random House India 2021

Copyright © Pankaj Dubey 2021

10 9 8 7 6 5 4 3 2 1

This is a work of fiction. Names, characters, places and incidents are either the
product of the author's imagination or are used fictitiously and any resemblance
to any actual person, living or dead, events or locales is entirely coincidental.

ISBN 9780143447955

Typeset in Bembo Std by Manipal Technologies Limited, Manipal
Printed at Thomson Press India Ltd, New Delhi

www.penguin.co.in

MIX
Paper
FSC   FSC® C010615

1

6 December 2002, Samachar Apartment Road, Delhi

An unexplained sadness grips him as soon as he opens his eyes. The premonition washes over him that it won't be a regular day. Something unpleasant is going to unfold. What that will be . . . he has no idea. Last night wasn't good either. The fight in the lane for the arrival of the ambulance and then, the silence filled with the wind hammering at his door. *So noisy and upsetting.* He tossed and turned in bed until late. Not that he sleeps well on other nights. But the darkness leading up to today has been different. It is darker. *What could be worse?*

He staggers out of bed and sticks his head out from the window. The sun—the little bit that is visible from here—looks the same. *Some blessing that is.* All else in his life has crumbled in the past decade. Shivam splashes water on his face and gets ready to face the day. He walks over to the part of the room that functions as his kitchen to make his tea and pack his lunch. He puts water to boil and chops two potatoes and two onions. Then he finds that he has run out of salt. *No sabzi then. Rotis and onions will have to do.*

Then it hits him again. *Today is no ordinary day.*

Someone bangs on his door. As he walks to it, the calendar on the side wall catches his eye. *6 December.* His heart stops. Almost.

There is more banging on the door. He hears it but doesn't respond. Instead, he crumbles to the floor, his head in his hands, fighting to block out the screams and cries tearing at him from within. After the noise outside stops, he gets up and showers and dresses for work. An hour later, Shivam revs up his motorcycle, acting normal. Helmet and knapsack on, he races down Delhi's sprawling roads before much of the city has woken up. He drives to the residential area of Lajpat Nagar and, parking his motorbike under a tree, walks to his tailoring boutique, a few metres away.

This has been his routine for the past ten years.

His muscular torso and easy, measured walk belie his tormented state of mind. A controlled existence—that's Shivam's mantra these days. He lets neither the demons inside nor the world outside affect him much.

'Designer sahib!' cries Munjal, his over-friendly neighbour, who runs a photocopy and computer printout unit from a hole in the wall in the opposite building. Shivam unlocks and rolls up the shutters of his tailoring shop as the morning news blares on Munjal's radio.

> *It's ten years today since the Babri Masjid was demolished. Still, we are nowhere near closure. Despite the issue dominating every single election and affecting crores of people across the country . . . the Supreme Court has yet again assigned one more date to the dispute petitions.*

Instead of stepping into his shop, Shivam turns towards Munjal's cubbyhole, pushes his arm in, and abruptly switches off the radio.

'Oy! That's my radio!' Munjal reminds the tailor.

But Shivam walks out, unapologetic.

A string of filthy swear-words follows. But, in his heart, Munjal knows that the tailor isn't a bully. He is generally gentle and non-interfering. He hardly ever speaks. What has happened today, he wonders. *'Babri* . . . Shivam doesn't want to hear that word again. Yet, he keeps getting reminded of it . . . twice since morning. First, that calendar. And now, the radio. *Hell!* Anger. Pain. Helplessness. They grip him all at once. He wants to blow up the whole damn universe . . . make it as empty as he feels. As he stands next to his machine, his back to Munjal's shop, his eyes begin to mist. He fights the tears. Fist clenched, he tells himself he won't let a teardrop fall. He has locked up his feelings so well for so long. He won't let them show now. No one will under. . .

His cell phone rings. Shivam is not surprised to get a call at this early hour. He fishes out the phone from his jeans pocket and puts it to his ear.

'Kitty!' Munjal hears the tailor exclaim. Shivam hardly has any calls. Who is calling him now? Maybe it's his girlfriend, the slightly chubby, almond-eyed Gujju woman who visits his boutique at least once a week. It is hard to concentrate on his customers while she is around. Her bouncing anklets—she wears three on her left leg—catch his eye every time.

'Not today,' Shivam's lips are drawn in a line.

How can he put her off? Munjal shakes his head. *Such a looker she is! Keen on the tailor too.* Yes, he has noticed and envies that cold-blooded fellow.

'Okay. Come,' he says with a sigh. As Shivam finally gives in, a smile stretches on Munjal's moustachioed lips. He has something to look forward to in his day.

Not so for the tailor, who throws his phone on the table and gets busy with his daily routine of measuring, drawing, cutting and sewing.

'Robot *kahin ka*,' mutters Munjal.

2

On a narrow stretch of road with residential apartments and a few shops on either side, between the row of sedate houses and grocery and stationery stores, Shivam's Aaina Boutique provides a colourful break, with its gaudy mannequins—slinky low-cut blouses in loud colours, tight salwar kurtas in garish patterns and cuts, and a special wedding range of lace and sequins catches the eyes of those passing by. Added to this is a constant stream of female customers of all shapes and sizes. The shop is quite an attraction.

Apart from Munjal, the watchman of the adjacent apartment complex also has his eye on the boutique, though that is not what he had been employed for. From the dressing up of the mannequins in their weekly outfit every Thursday morning to their disrobing Wednesday nights before pack up—they miss nothing. Munjal sees the tailor tuck, pin and smoothen out the blouse on the mannequin's frame till it sits snug. When Shivam drapes a sari or lehenga tightly round the plastic doll, the guard expels a breath he had been holding.

Shivam, though, seems to go about his business without a shred of emotion. At thirty-one, he looks much younger and more attractive than his envious neighbour Munjal.

He does not change his facial expression for anyone. Not even for the flesh-and-blood beauties flocking to his boutique—little girls with their mothers for an occasional dress, young girls on the brink of puberty for tight-fitting suits and backless cholis, buxom women requesting him for the latest in blouses. All through it, his face stays impassive. Come festive season, the shop is heaven, overflowing with angels. He measures them, standing close. Seeing them, and yet not looking. Both Munjal and the guard sit drooling from their distant perches.

Kitty arrives in a sleeveless mauve top and fitted denim capris. It is December and still no sleeves! She puts Munjal in the heat. Kitty flails her hands as she speaks. She looks more excited than usual. She pats Shivam on the shoulder, tries to get close to him.

Munjal grumbles to himself as he can't hear her.

Shivam stands before Kitty, his eyes and ears open, but mind elsewhere. She snaps her fingers to get his attention.

Embarrassed, Shivam tunes in to her again.

'Is something wrong, Shivu?' she asks.

He shakes his head. No

'You're game for this *na*?' she continues. 'We'll pucca scorch the ramp.'

Shivam is in two minds.

Kitty gets this. So before he can say no, she unleashes the full blueprint of her idea. 'Twelve ensembles to begin with . . . this for the Kolkata showing . . . Next, we go to Hyderabad. And . . . ' she grips his arm then, 'if they like us, Shivu . . . and I know they will . . . there's no stopping us then . . . ' Into his ears, she whispers, 'Orders, orders . . . only orders, then!' she says triumphantly, her eyes twinkling with the dream.

Kitty, so ambitious and talented. Shivam wants to dream with her. Make those dreams come true. But he stops. He is feeling low, he tells her.

'Why didn't you say this before?' chirps Kitty. '*Chalo*, my treat. We'll have chole bhature . . . even I've not eaten anything since . . . '

'*Arrey*, I didn't mean that!' Shivam pulls back as she begins dragging him out of the shop. 'You took me literally.'

Kitty's cell phone rings, stalling their battle for the moment.

Munjal is enjoying the show. So is the guard.

Kitty ends her call. Shivam is about to decline her again, firmly this time, when he catches Munjal ogling. Not wanting to provide more entertainment for Munjal or the guard, he lets her take him for chole bhature or whatever . . .

* * *

Dipping his fluffy bhatura into the spicy chola curry, Shivam considers the girl squeezed in next to him, shoulder to shoulder, on the tiny bench in Ramlal's famous Lajpat Nagar dhaba.

'Have with this,' she says, spooning pickled onions into his mouth.

Shivam almost chokes. It isn't the onions. It is her. He does not know how to handle her.

She is close to him and yet not close. And he does not have the . . .

She offers him another spoonful, cutting into his thoughts.

'Wait . . . I'll have . . . I will.'

'No,' she puckers her lips into a pout. 'Can't I?'

He lets her feed him and talk about all that plays on her mind and she goes on and on with her idea map, drawing out the future in detail, hers, his, and theirs.

'Shivu,' she murmurs as he escorts her to her scooty, twenty minutes later. 'We are a good fit . . . and not just in work, I mean.' With that she zips away, leaving him thinking about what she has just said. For a few minutes, Shivam just stands there confused, in a bind over whether to work with her or not. Still undecided, he slowly walks back to his shop and picks up work from where he had left it.

The day rolls on. Once the sun reaches its zenith, Shivam gets up from his sewing machine and moves to the shop counter that doubles up as his work table. Neatly dressed in an ochre-yellow checked shirt tucked into chestnut-brown trousers, held in place by a narrow black belt, he looks dapper despite his unassuming air. His hair falls on his forehead as he bends over the counter to measure a piece of cloth. He jerks his head up to throw back the flick covering his eyes.

If only he could throw back the years in the same way . . .

If he could turn the clock back ten years . . .

Ten years since the mosque came down, ending with it everything and everyone that mattered to Shivam. Yes, everything . . . everything, but Babloo, that music-mad friend of his. Shivam laughs at the irony of Babloo being left behind. Even in the netherworld, they must not have the courage to bear the fellow's shrill singing.

Shivam's laugh attracts Munjal's curiosity and he gets off his stool and walks across to the boutique.

'Chacha?' Shivam asks, unsure why the middle-aged man has suddenly chosen to bless his shop.

'What Chacha, Chacha . . . do you have nothing else to say?'

'No, no . . . it's not like that,' says Shivam a bit embarrassed, his eyes still on the pattern he has been drawing with chalk on the fabric. 'Just that I'm not good at talking to people.'

'Not good, my foot! With that Kitty of yours, you are faster than *Rajdhani!*' counters Munjal, referring to the superfast train.

Not bothering to reply, Shivam spreads the cut-piece fabric he folded earlier to mark out a blouse pattern. With the eagle-eyed neighbour watching him keenly, he checks the armhole length and shoulder-to-shoulder measurement once again. He then cuts out the front and back shapes and arranges them on his table for sewing, not forgetting the pleats and the straight bands on which hooks will be fixed.

'Wow!'

Before Shivam can stop him, the photocopy manager picks up the front cut-out of a blouse and dangles it in wonder in front of him, imagining how it will look when ready.

No, he can't allow this! Shivam pulls the piece back from his hands and looks angrily at the neighbour. He can't just walk over to his boutique any time he feels like and touch his things and get turned on at the thought of the customer!

'Please don't disturb me,' he says firmly. 'If even one measurement goes wrong, the whole piece will get spoilt.'

'It's for Taneja madam, na?' asks Munjal, ignoring his statement, 'I'm sure . . . it seems her size.'

'Come, let's have some tea,' offers Shivam, wanting to divert his middle-aged visitor's attention. Throwing an arm around his shoulders, he leads the man out of his shop.

Barely a few metres away, under a tarpaulin shack, the chai wallah conducts brisk business. As the two sit cradling their tiny glasses of hot, milky, ginger chai, Munjal laments, 'Why can't we do this more often?'

Because this isn't what he wants to do. With Munjal, or with anyone for that matter.

He can hear Munjal growl irately. 'It's always the machine . . . your ma'ams . . . and back to the sewing machine. It seems nothing else exists!'

Yes, accepts Shivam. *It's always the machine.* For the machine is all he has left in his life.

3

Ayodhya, 1992

Even back then, the sewing machine had been at the centre of all his disputes with his family. His mother had one and he enjoyed seeing her work on it. If there was any mending to be done, he would happily help. Soon, he was not just mending but also experimenting, as he tried to sew all kinds of things—pillow covers, curtains, dresses—newer designs and patterns constantly playing on his mind. All this when his Baba, Mahant Avdhesh, the head priest of the temple at the Ram Janmabhoomi site, venerated by all in this temple town of Ayodhya, was looking to groom him into his able successor.

'Shivam!'

The booming voice sent Shivam scurrying into the mahant's room.

His father was arranging the thali—a huge, copper plate with a brass lamp, camphor, vermilion and more—for the mangal-aarti ritual the next day, when the lit-up ghee-soaked wicks would be waved ceremoniously in offering to the gods.

'For a change, make yourself useful,' he bellowed on seeing his son.

As Shivam went about fetching whatever his priest father demanded next, the old man didn't hold himself back:

'Just running around here and there won't do . . . twenty-one year old and not one mangal aarti I can trust you to lead . . . *mahant ka beta* . . . *par genda phool ho* . . . you're just for decoration!

Being likened to marigold blossoms used to deck up the idols was supposed to be derogatory, but Shivam didn't find it so. The yellow, orange, multi-hued balls of petals, which were stitched into garlands and temple over-hangings or fashioned into bracelets and anklets for the divine, had always fired his imagination.

So, he smiled. His grumbling father noticed that tiny gesture and launched a tirade.

He thought the boy was mocking him. Picking up the stick that he kept in the room to scare away monkeys, he grabbed his offspring by the collar of his fancy turquoise shirt and started beating him. Thwack . . . thwack . . .

'Aaaah! Shivam yelped, jumping in pain as he tried to dodge the stick. All that *mudgal* swinging he had done in the akhara next door came to naught. Same as the monkeys, he ran around yelping in pain. Clearly his gym trainer was wrong when he promised him that working out with the five-kilo Indian club would turn him into *Vajra*.

'Stop!' His mother rushed in and wedged herself between the two men. 'He's just twenty-one, why do you forget!'

'He's forgetting, not me,' hit back the seething priest, the stick still trembling in his hand. 'Twenty-one! Yet up to no good.'

Shivam found his voice once the stick was gone. 'Your good is not my good, Baba.'

That brought the mahant stomping up to him again, spitting fire.

'*Kal ka launda*, you'll teach me . . . I, Mahant Avdhesh . . . I . . . ' he stammered in rage. 'Ministers come to me to set their lives right. I . . . I do their puja. And you, my own blood . . . you dare defy me.'

'Hear him out,' his mother pleaded, shielding her son from the mahant's wrath.

'Don't be a priest if you don't want to. Set up a prasad shop. Selling divine oblations brings good money. And you'll be blessed too.'

'No. You know, that's not what I want to do.'

'Then what you want to do . . . stick your head in ladies' blouses with that Muslim *darzi*!' The mahant thundered, drawing menacingly close again.

Shivam's mother holds her son, dreading the answer and the fight it would spark.

'What's wrong in it . . . even Hindus wear blouses . . . and Murshid Mia can teach me what no Hindu tailor can.'

Pushing aside his wife, the mahant slapped his son.

'Dharma! You dare speak against your dharma! Muslims are good for you now, huh?'

Numbed by the slap, Shivam was not in a state to respond.

'It's the hormones,' the mahant lambasted him, breathing heavily. 'They're driving you insane.'

The priest's wife dragged her husband to a corner, away from her son. He needed the distance to cool down and come to terms with the fact that his legacy would drown, whether he liked it or not.

'If you have the drive to become something,' continued the priest from the corner, 'come with me. Come for the

Rath Yatra. We will go around the country in a chariot, like Lord Ram, preaching the Hindu dharma. That, my son, will pump you up like nothing else . . . come!'

Shivam looked at his dhoti-kurta clad, head-anointed, seer of a father straight in the eye and declared, 'Dharma is not that important to me.'

Before the old man could digest the statement, he left the room.

* * *

That wasn't the end of the argument.

'Remember who you are and where you're born,' reminded his mother, later that evening while he was helping her stack up the billowing costumes and over-hangings of the goddesses.

'I'm different. Can't you see that,' argued Shivam.

'And how are you different,' threw the mahant, who had just entered the storeroom.

'Baba,' Shivam tried to explain, 'Like you dress your deities in silk and in flowers and vermilion . . . ' he paused, 'I want to dress up girls in a hundred hues, and in cuts that cling to their skin like raindrops.'

'How dare you!' The old man began frothing at the mouth and shaking. It took him time to calm down and hit out. 'Devi ma will scald your tongue, you sinner! 'You put street girls over *devi-devtas*! *Kalanki*!'

Again, his wife tried to hold him back. She was scared things had gone too far.

The mahant was trembling. How could his son talk this way? How could he disrespect gods and goddesses? Even talking like this was sinning. How could he? 'I must have messed up somewhere to deserve this . . . yes, something in my puja has gone wrong . . .' he muttered to himself.

His overwrought state brought tears to his wife's eyes. Shivam couldn't bear this. He rushed to his mother and gathered her in a hug. Only to be shrugged off.

As the boy walked out, he heard his mother suggest, 'Do a havan, mahantji, the sacred flame will remove these clouds from his mind.'

And the mahant agreed. 'Yes, praying to the holy fire is the only way now. Ram *lalla* will swing him back to the right path.'

Shivam shook his head. They would never understand him.

* * *

'Now, who will get cervical?' sniggers someone, jolting the boy out of his past.

Shivam looks up from his machine. Munjal has walked into the shop again and caught the tailor sitting at his machine, daydreaming and shaking his head at past events. He gives this over-friendly neighbour a defeated look, a hint for him to leave.

'I'm going, I'm going . . . don't worry,' says Munjal, backing away.

The day drones on. The honking of cars that want to whiz past but cannot vie with the call of vendors pushing their carts laden mostly with fruit and vegetables or winter delights like boiled sweet potato with a sprinkling of dark spicy powder and a tangy squeeze of lemon. There are the autorickshaw wallahs and the bicycle-borne, not to forget a perennial stream of pedestrians who nonchalantly drift onto the road from the side pavements.

But Shivam is hard at work. This outside noise doesn't bother him; the noise inside of him is too loud.

4

There has been a steady flow of business since early morning—mostly petticoats and blouses. Wedding season sees a spike in demand for these. And so goes half the day. Drafting. Cutting. Sewing. Measuring up new customers. Listening to the whining of the older ones who have put on weight and need him to loosen the fit. Sari blouses to lehenga cholis to patialas and kurtis . . . almost all within the five-kilometre radius come to him for stitching and fitting.

A woman has brought her daughter along for a kurta. 'Masterji, don't make it too tight. Just give a taper so she looks slimmer.'

'No, don't listen to Mummy,' counters the fourteen-year-old. 'I want it hugging . . . else I won't wear.'

Shivam measures the teenager closely even as he reassures the mother with an understanding nod, checking an all-out war from breaking out in his shop.

'No, it won't be loose,' he confirms to the girl before she leaves. Small bulges mushrooming on a once-lean frame have made the teenager insecure. Shivam knows exactly how to minimize these form defects with flattering cuts. That's what draws the belles and *maha* bellies to his shop. At times, they barely leave him time to break for lunch or tea.

He sighs as he pulls out his steel tiffin box from the shelf below the counter and takes this customer-free-moment to eat. He looks at his work as he eats. Shivam has been working on a sharara set with extra ruffles and pleats to fill out a scrawny frame. What if he had the skill to add girth to his sunken life too or use the scissors to snip off life's unsavoury bits? Only on cloth, he was king . . . sewing to make the ends meet, literally,

Just then a silver Honda City drives up to his shop entrance, breaking into his thoughts. The driver rolls down his window, cranes out his head, hands over a polythene bag with hurried instructions.

'Ma'am's blouses for loosening. Six of them,' he barks, raising his voice over the loud honking from traffic held up behind him. 'The green one is the right fit . . . use that. And I'll collect it all tomorrow.'

'No. Not Friday . . . I can't . . . '

'Tomorrow,' cuts in the driver. 'She wants tomorrow only. Will pay extra.' And he rolls up his window as drivers behind him on the narrow lane are impatient and irritated.

As Shivam opens the packet to count the clothes inside, the Honda window rolls down again. 'I forgot, there's a kurta also . . . loosen it as much as you can. And also, the lace is coming off . . . just mend that.' The driver does not dare to wait any more as the honking gets insistent.

'Arrey, hear the charges at least . . .' Shivam calls out, wanting to count out the pieces before the driver and quote accordingly. But the car is gone. Shivam empties out the contents of the bag on his work table.

Four blouses slip out. A kurta follows . . . an orange Banarsi silk . . . More stuff tumbles out . . . but Shivam's heart has stopped. His fingers caress the fabric . . .

Flaming orange. Iridescent. The colour of the gulmohar in full bloom. Shivam rubs his eyes, blinded by the bright hue. Inside him, there is a sudden vacuum—like all the air has been sucked out. The present . . . the thoughts of another day . . . none of them exist. Even the shop fades away . . .

Leaving only the orange silk in his hand and it takes him back to the past.

The mahant was caught in the beauty of the Banarsi cut-piece he had placed in his son's hands.

'Feel its texture, so rich, and the colour, so brilliant!' the old man gushed.

For once, even Shivam agreed. That's a fine piece of fabric. Classic handloom silk with flower embroidery. Its silken yarns woven into an enviable shine.

'Here, take this too.'

Shivam reached out for the shiny silver-gold bundle—zari brocade, made of gold threads painstakingly wound over silk yarns.

'See how the zari adds to the lustre of the cloth?' pointed out the priest. 'Apt for someone you worship.'

Bowled by its brilliance, the boy kept nodding, unaware of where the conversation was leading.

'So adorn her with it . . . make the goddess glow with your talent.'

Shivam turned over the cloth in his hands, seeing it with new eyes.

The mahant continued, 'Stitch for the divine. And she might forgive you . . . your waywardness.'

Yes, his father was right, Shivam acknowledged. *This was fit only for a goddess. And meant to be stitched by him. He would do it. Work on it like it was worship.*

As he left the room with the unexpected gift, his father's words followed, 'You'll be of some use to her even on your wrongful path . . .'

Tears sting his eyes. Something comes into view. Shivam tries to see through the haze of tears. It is a petticoat.

He finds it difficult to focus on the pale pink after the brilliant orange.

'Masterji, the length has to be cut by two inches.'

The words bring him sharply back into the present. A customer is in his shop for alteration of her petticoat.

Hastily wiping his tears and shoving the orange kurta under the counter, the tailor accepts the pink petticoat and marks out the length to be shortened. The customer continues talking, explaining what she wants and Shivam nods. Pink, blue, green, yellow . . . the colours keep changing. Someone brings in a *lehenga* he had stitched earlier, another wants a few blouses stitched, then there's a white kurta to be made.

He is in another world today, performing his task with a mechanical speed. He attacks the pending pile of clothes first, then moves to the pieces he was unable to refuse that day. There is an energy about him.

He's got to finish it all . . . today . . . now.

At sunset, he rolls down the shutters. The noise of the metal crashing down startles the guard on the opposite perch. He swings around to check. *What the hell! Why has the darzi shut down so early today?* He checks his watch. *Only 6 p.m.!* Not once has the tailor downed shutters before 10 p.m. *And where is the human glacier?* He can't see the fellow. He is neither outside the shop nor in the lane. *He couldn't have melted . . . had he?*

Streetlights have not yet been lit. The shutter is not fully down and he can see a glow at the bottom. Even the lock is missing. The guard's keen eye is trained to miss nothing. Someone is inside, he deduces in a flash and hurries over to investigate. Munjal joins him. Pushing the shutter up a few inches, the watchman bends to peep in and finds the young man at his worktable, pedalling furiously on his sewing machine. The guard raises the shutter some more. Munjal squeezes his bulk in and walks up to the tailor.

'Is this your new style?' he asks.

'I did not want any disturbance. I've got to finish this quickly.'

Munjal peeks in. It is a yellow blouse with net sleeves. He watches. This one's almost done. A minute later, the tailor folds and stacks it aside and scoops up another, a purple one this time.

Both Munjal and the guard stand watching for a few minutes. Both feel something is amiss. Knowing the fellow is unlikely to confide in them, they turn to leave.

'You okay na?' checks Munjal, before downing the shutter again.

Shivam nods, without looking up. His fingers are pulling apart the side seam to loosen the blouse.

An hour and a half later, he is done. As he locks up and leaves, the watchman sees him go. He is carrying the tiffin and another packet that he stuffs into his shirt before whizzing off on the motorcycle. The guard stares in disbelief. Everything about this tailor is different today.

Back in his rented accommodation, Shivam is in no mood to eat, clean or do anything that needs to be done.

He sprawls on the bed with his packet. He empties it out on himself, letting the orange kurta flow out of it, and with it, the tangerine memories—*a riverfront, a boat on the gently undulating waters, steps, someone racing up, cycling past the bazaar, running up to the gates, waiting, watching, watching her and living.*

The radiant fabric spreads across his face, Shivam inhales deeply, feels its silkiness against his cheeks. He soaks in its welcome warmth and loses himself completely . . .

* * *

He was on a boat, on the Sarayu in Ayodhya, bobbing up and down its mossy green waters, a basket of flowers bouncing alongside. He passed the many temples lining the riverbank, some dating back to ancient times when the mighty King Vikramaditya ruled.

Scorched by the rising sun, the Sarayu flowed bravely, mindful of its role in history. Winter, though late that year, was tiptoeing round the corner. The pilgrims dipping in the muddy waters for salvation could feel the drop in temperature.

Unmindful of it all, Shivam jumped out of the boat and raced up the slippery steps of the bank, through the masses and the mess to enter a Shiva temple with his basket of marigolds. He quickly said his prayers and skipped out.

The early morning breeze hit his face, playing through his hair as if admiring this lithe twenty-one-year-old, pulsating with life and energy as he scampered up to the lane behind the ghat, where he had kept his bicycle inside a sweet shop. The shop was packed with people lined up for a breakfast of round, fluffy puris and spicy alu sabzi, followed by sweet, brown halwa that simmered temptingly in a cauldron.

But Shivam didn't care. The aroma didn't tempt him one bit. Wheeling out his bicycle, he pedalled furiously down the narrow lanes, weaving past chai stalls and decrepit havelis. He stopped only at Murshid Mia's tailoring shop. This was where he was training to be the biggest *karigar* that the town, if not the state, had seen. Yes, Murshid Mia had magic in his hands, everyone in the twin towns of Ayodhya and Faizabad knew this. His agreeing to take on Shivam as an apprentice was as big as getting the Filmfare Awards he watches on TV, without exception, every year.

Three hours whizzed past. Designing, pattern making, cutting, stitching and fitting—it was all a fine art. When you're doing what your heart desires, time ceases to exist.

Shivam's heart skipped a beat as he remembered that someone was waiting for him, at a distance that would take him at least twenty minutes to cover. This someone was closer than anyone ever had been or could be to him. For the first time, he smiled.

He rushed out and reached his destination, gasping. Then, leaning his cycle against the neem tree, he walked up farther and called out, 'Babloo!'

The boy lounging near the gates of the girls' higher secondary school did not respond.

5

'Babloo!'
Still no response.

Annoyed, Shivam put his hands into the boy's pocket and switched off whatever was playing on the Walkman lodged inside.

Babloo turned around and saw him.

'Bhaiya,' he said, 'it's your love, right? Then why am I the one waiting here and sweating it out?'

'Arrey, one day I get late and the sun has already killed our friendship?'

'No, Bhaiya, that was not what I was trying to say. I was only . . .'

Shivam cut him. 'You know na. I've just started going to Murshid Mia from this week?'

'But I've been standing here for forty minutes!' Babloo protested.

'So?' Shivam gave it back. 'You would've won the KBC in this time, huh?'

Babloo looked at him darkly. Everyone was watching *Kaun Banega Crorepati* (*KBC*), the high-stakes TV quiz show, those days.

'You right . . . ' Shivam suddenly felt bad for his friend, 'I've been wasting your time.'

'Forget it, Bhaiya, come, look,' said Babloo, and winked, hauling himself up the gate. This back gate of the Mahila Mahavidyalaya stayed abandoned at this late hour, when the school was about to get over. The front gate guard did make rounds to check it during the day though.

The two boys made haste and climbed up the back gate to land on the other side, ran over to the water tank looming before them, and clambered up to get an unrestricted view of the school's playground beyond.

The girls were playing kho kho today. It was their free time, after classes, before the bell rang to signal it was time to go home. The boys knew the schedule. Every Tuesday, Thursday and Friday, the twelfth standard girls got this time off. Some loitered, others played games. It was always kho kho.

Most of the girls were sitting in formation, some were running. In the blue salwar kameez uniform, they looked like bluebirds chasing each other. A few of them were in burqas.

'That one.' Shivam pointed out his girl from all those sitting and running.

'Sure?' Babloo sounded sceptical for she was completely cloaked in a burqa. And not one but four more girls were running around in burqas.

'Sure! I can pick her in a billion,' replied Shivam. 'Anywhere.'

'But how?'

Just then his girl spotted them.

'Her eyes,' whispered Shivam. 'Her blue eyes . . . there is an ocean in them.'

Babloo shook his head.

'How can you tell from up here whether they are black or blue?'

'I know.'

'How does it feel, Bhaiya?'

'What?'

Shivam was only half-listening, his mind and heart on the girl as she ran. Stopped. And turned with lightning speed, seeing another girl get up to chase. Changing course . . . slipping . . .

'Aaaaa . . .' his heart cried out.

Babloo quickly pulled his friend down, behind the advertisement banner erected on the tank. What if someone heard them and came checking! Not even that resourceful cousin he had—the one who worked in this school—could save them then.

They crouched low . . . waiting . . . for footsteps that signal trouble . . . .

But even as they hid, Shivam couldn't help but peep out, to see if she was okay.

Seeing her running, still trying to dodge, he smiled. *His girl . . . always a winner!* And then she stumbled once more. Something had caught her attention.

'Shit!'

Shivam slid away again.

It was him. She had seen him. Maybe she had heard him too, when he cried out before. And that meant . . . Shivam shivered as it hit him . . . *that meant she too had her eye on him . . . on the tank . . . on them . . . His sudden reappearance from hiding had made her stop, and lose.*

'Babloo, she knows . . . she knows we're here!' Shivam screamed excitedly. 'And . . . and it affects her.'

Babloo whacked his friend playfully, trying to curb Shivam's excitement. At least his friend had not screamed this time. That would have exposed their hiding place. As they crouched behind the banner on the water tank, Shivam could not take his eyes away from the ground. *What was it about this girl that made him take such risks?*

Then as if Babloo had heard him, he nudged Shivam again and repeated his question. 'Arrey, tell na . . . how does it feel . . . all this love-*shove*?'

'I feel . . . I feel alive and dead at the same time.'

Babloo looked blankly at him. 'Huh?'

'Not seeing her kills me . . . and then one look from her, just one, and I want to live forever.'

'Bhaiya, you're turning into a dreamer.'

'You will too, Babloo . . . when love hits you.'

'No way,' denied his friend swiftly. 'Music is enough for me.'

'Music feeds on love,' Shivam threw back at him. 'Every song Nusrat saheb sings, he sings for us.' Then he sighed, 'Arrey, I can flunk twelfth again . . . just for one smile from her.'

Babloo was impressed. Not clearing the school final *had* almost killed his friend.

As the game wound up and the girls lined up to go indoors, his friend's girl in the burqa looked one last time in their direction, before joining the others.

'Did you see that? She knows!' Shivam squeezed Babloo's arm and pointed out, jubilantly.

'You're a hero, Bhaiya,' acknowledged Babloo, as they jumped down the tank and went back the way they had come.

'What you want?' asked Shivam then, not falling for the 'hero' bait.

'No, Bhaiya. Why would I want anything at all?' But a minute later, he confessed, 'Those new cassettes are out . . . the ones I was telling you about yesterday, and I'm short on cash.' He looked down as they walked out.

Shivam laughed, 'Okay, so this is what makes you hang out with me!'

'No. Never!' Babloo said with a pained look. 'Let it be. I don't want the cassettes.'

'Arrey, I know.' Shivam put his hand on his friend's shoulder. 'How crazy you are about music. I know. I'll get you the cassettes.'

'Bhaiya, don't you ever question our friendship,' His face was sombre, 'I will do anything for you . . . anything.'

Shivam laughed it off as the two cycled over to the front gate of the girls' school, to begin the second phase of their watch.

A stream of girl students flowed out. It was a flurry of blue kurtas and excited chattering faces, their cotton chunnis dancing behind them, with their bouncing school bags. Both an ice-cream wallah and a makeshift chaat food stall did brisk business as a gaggle marched over to them excitedly. A number of burqas fluttered out too, billowing in black or blue. Shivam sought out that one blue wave he had deemed his own. He looked past these cloaks for that singular beauty . . . the one that no veil could hide.

And there she was . . . surrounded by her salwar kameez-clad friends, weaving her way out. A pep in her step . . . half-skipping as she walked, her mind running on hundred different tracks as she made her way to the gate. He watched her wave to someone, call out to another, and then get startled by a stray cat that crossed her way. She lit up all his senses . . . even half-asleep he would know it was her . . . of that he was sure.

Nearing the gate, she got self-conscious. He saw her growing less chirpy and walking on her toes a bit, maybe, trying to look taller. The gang paused at the gate. Seeing the boys, the girls poked their burqa friend, passed comments and started giggling. She continued walking but pretended she hadn't heard them. Shivam held his breath as she drew closer, within inches of him. Before she crossed the road to reach her rickshaw, their eyes locked. For one brief, timeless moment. And he drowned in the depth of all that he saw in them.

She saw him drowning. And let him. She knew he didn't want to be saved. Her eyelashes fluttered. And they connected, needing no words.

In that crowded lane, she saw only him. And he, her. The cacophony of horns, traffic and people reached their ears but didn't register. It was as if they were suspended in each other's magic.

'Wait, Bhaiya, I'll get Monu's Luna . . . you go after her on that bike,' said Babloo, getting up from his perch.

Her eyes widened at this. Shivam held his friend back with a hand, not breaking eye contact with her. And then she was gone. On the rickshaw she'd hailed.

'Aaina!' he called out to her once she was gone.

Babloo sighed. Watching it on screen was one thing . . . up close, love was a painful business.

'I was getting the Luna. Why did you stop me?'

'Your sister knows her. Can you not fix one meeting,' he asked as if he hadn't heard his friend.

'Today only, *maa kasam*,' swore Babloo. 'I'll talk to her.'

Shivam sighed, got on his bike and cycled away. He was singing a popular romantic number.

6

Aaina stepped out of the rickshaw and plunged straight into an argument.

'Is it biting you?' Naved said sarcastically as he watched his sister pull off her burqa the minute she stepped inside the house.

'Wear it and see na, you'll know!' she retorted.

Ammi left the spice jar she was filling in the kitchen and entered the hall breathing fire. 'Aaina, mind how you talk to your brother!'

'Why, Ammi? Why do you always take his side?' Aaina said.

'Naved is right. You're getting too disrespectful. Abbu won't like it.'

'No one likes anything I do!' Aaina pulled her niqab back in anger and sat pouting, refusing to eat the khana Ammi offered.

Naved smirked. This was the daily drama of the Farooqui household.

'Girls should stay like girls,' Ammi mouthed for the hundredth time to her rebellious seventeen-year-old, even as she threw back the girl's veil and fed her forcefully.

'I was feeling hot, Ammi,' Aaina told her mother once her obnoxious brother was out of earshot.

'I know. But you can't answer back to men like this . . . they won't take it.'

'Men!' Aaina rolled her eyes and tried to imagine a grown-up version of that monstrous younger brother of hers. 'Ammi, he'll never grow up.'

'*Chup!*' Ammi silenced her.

'He won't,' she insisted, 'because Abbu won't let him.'

Ammi's eyes welled up with tears. Her daughter reminded her so much of herself, but aeons ago.

'Mind your words,' Naved said, walking into the mother-daughter conversation.

'You mind yourself . . . you need to!' Aaina gave it back.

'Lower your gaze, when you talk to me!' the boy mimicked his Abbu, riling up his sister even more.

'That's for boys failing twice in one grade. *You* should look down.'

'Aaina!' Ammi stopped her daughter from battling further. But the damage was done.

'You wait, I'll crush that crown you've got on your head,' her brother slammed his fist in anger. Aaina had topped her class, so her jibe that he had failed stung. 'College . . . now you see who lets you go . . . you wait now . . . ' Naved threatened her, standing right before her and emphasized what he had said with an exaggerated shake of his neck.

Aaina was almost in tears. College, education, freedom . . . how she craved these. This grudging, useless brother of hers would now go fill Abbu's ears with rubbish, making her case impossible.

Naved was not finished. He had more bones to pick.

'Why have you not removed that nail polish . . . Abbu told you na?'

Now Ammi sent him out of the room.

Aaina looked down at her nails, painted blue to match her eyes. Very few things were not haram for a girl, nail paint being one of the few things her religion did not forbid. And how she treasured these little indulgences that were permitted—a miniature, flower-shaped wooden brooch to the side of her burqa, just where the niqab fell, touching her shoulders. She even dared to walk out in high heels sometimes. These were tiny, harmless adornments, proclaiming her womanhood and making her stand out from the rest. Things, *he* noticed, thought Aaina, and smiled. Her mother gave her a questioning look.

'Nothing.' Aaina shook her head.

Unconvinced, Ammi looked at her closely. Ammi was one person who could read into her heart. Scared, she skipped to hug her mother, hiding her face in Ammi's ample bosom.

No, it wouldn't do to let her into her thoughts. Ammi would not be happy and would bar her from stepping out of the house alone.

She could not risk that. Never. Her admirer, his flowers, his daily visits, all of it would have to stay a secret.

In one emotional moment, two years ago, Ammi had mentioned how she loved dancing and would go for classes secretly. She had even performed with boys on stage. Then, her parents found out and got her engaged overnight. They married her off to Abbu soon after. And what had she become? Aaina sneaked up a glance, even as her arms stayed around her mother's girth. Listless. That's how Ammi's eyes looked. Not expressive, alive, and burning with passion as a dancer's should be. As Ammi gently disengaged and walked away to answer her son's call, Aaina discerned in her mother's gait a rhythm and grace that she had thought of as regular. Yes, it was there. Dead, but there.

Watching Ammi pamper the youngest male member of the household, Aaina mourned the passing away of the passion. Ammi now looked like a pillar, polished to reflect the whims, fancies and beliefs of her husband. A husband who got swayed by whatever was trending in the community at that particular moment, like that illogical fatwa against wearing nail polish by a random cleric a few months ago. Abbu had been after Aaina about the nail polish since. Sometimes, Abbu acted progressively. It was in one such instance that he decided to give both his children the best education available in their city. At most other times though, he went by rusty beliefs, framing ever-new rules, making them binding on the family, especially on its female members. Ammi weathered it calmly, striking a harmonious balance with her domestic responsibilities.

Aaina refused to become another Ammi. She prayed and believed in all the teachings. But she also believed in herself . . . her thoughts . . . her desires—the sweet and sour churning that went on inside her. It confused her at times but also made her sing and skip and smile so often.

So she fished out the tiny bottle of nail paint from the drawer in her corner cupboard and began touching up her nails.

'Ouch, your nail dug in!' yelped Shivam, pulling his head away.

'So stay still na.'

A soft whack on the back nudged Shivam to sit up again. And ma resumed the head massage. She was doing his *champi*—pouring hot coconut oil onto his scalp and rubbing it in by pressing and drumming her palms rhythmically on his head. But her boy just could not sit in one place—turning to talk to Babloo, bending to look at something, picking up another thing. It was a heroic effort to get the oil in without it dripping all over his face and shirt. In all that clapping and stroking to coax the oil in, she now needed to ensure that her nails did not bite his skin.

'Have you fixed the meeting?' Shivam asked his friend as his mother cupped her palm, poured oil in and rubbed the back of his head.

He got no reply. He had to turn his head to find Babloo lost in a world of his own—head bobbing in tandem with whatever was playing on his Walkman. Shivam leaned across and yanked off the headphones.

'What man!'

'What . . . what?' Shivam countered. 'Get lost! And take that damned gadget out with you.'

'Arrey, Bhaiya, I won't use it,' Babloo promised. 'But you've got to hear this remix. I got it done myself, in the studio.'

Shivam dismissed it with a desultory wave of his hand.

'Once, Bhaiya, once. Just listen to it once. I promise you won't want to hear anything else!'

'Chup *bey*! You say this for every new song you get.'

'You don't take me seriously na,' Babloo whined, 'I'll show you . . . few years, and I'll show you.'

Shivam sniggered.

Babloo ignored him and chimed on. 'My future's in music. Only music.'

'And mine in blue eyes . . . only blue eyes.'

The words were out even before Shivam realized he had uttered them.

'Blue eyes?' His mother caught on immediately, her hands slowing down.

'Shivam is talking of Shiva . . . ' started Babloo, trying to deflect her.

But she cut him short. 'Yes, I'm sure he looks deep into god's eyes.'

'Arrey, my ma is smarter than you, *lallu*!' Shivam laughed.

'But not my son.'

'Meaning?'

'Meaning . . . he chooses the wrong path . . . always,' said his mother.

'The one who listens to Nusrat Ali can never be wrong,' declared Babloo.

'Again, Muslim. Even in songs, why it has to be a Muslim?' She gets annoyed. 'What's it with you boys? Have you forgotten you are Hindu?'

'Don't talk like Baba,' Shivam said.

'Gulshan Kumar's bhajans won't burn your ears,' she persisted.

'But they will fry his heart for sure,' replied Babloo, winking at his friend.

'Baba was right. I should look for an *achchi* girl . . . she'll set him right.' Ma's pronouncement riled up Shivam.

'And who'll feed and clothe this achchi girl of yours? You? Baba?'

'Thank God! At least you realize she will be your responsibility,' his mother said, folding her hands. 'Soon, very soon, this stitching *ka bhoot* will also vanish. Craze, that's all it is.'

'You vanish now, Ma. My skull's cracking with all this achchi talk,' Shivam swung away from her grasp and jumped up. Just managing to save the oil bottle from being knocked down by him, his mother hoisted herself up.

Back in his room and out of earshot, Shivam accosted Babloo again.

'Did you fix the meeting or not?'

'Arrey, Bhaiya, have some patience.'

'*Abey*, Gulshan Kumar *ke* clone, one more gyan you give . . . I'll remix you into a Bhojpuri number.'

'Bhaiya, have faith. I've told Babita di to fix it,' Babloo said. 'She'll confirm tomorrow.'

'Tomorrow . . . how will I sleep tonight?'

Babloo shook his head and left his friend sighing.

7

It was Monday. A new week had started, and with it, something new began for Aaina. After the classes, she did not hail a rickshaw to take her straight home. Instead, she opted to walk up to the sweet shop that doubled as a restaurant, with her friend Rehana.

Even her burqa was of a different colour—silver-grey with a lacy hijab veil. Rehana was cloaked in the regular blue. The girls occupied a table at the back. The sweet shop boasted of only six tables. Babloo was sitting at the next one, diagonally opposite to them. With him was Shivam, fidgeting more than sitting.

No one spoke at either table.

Four-five minutes crawled by.

Babloo decided to change this. He opened his mouth.

'I'm Babloo. Babita didi, my sister . . . she called up na . . .'

Shivam pinched him hard under the table.

'Ouch!'

He took over.

'Shivam. Hi! I'm Shivam.'

But that was all he managed. An awkward silence descended over the tables once again.

Aaina and Shivam sat facing each other, saying nothing.

Rehana decided to perk things up by leaving.

'Toilet,' she said to her friend, who held on to her robe.

Babloo took the cue. 'Forgot to lock my cycle,' he blabbered, jumping to follow her out, wanting to give the love birds a chance.

Shivam sat mulling over what to say.

Babloo returned to whisper into his ear, so loudly that Aaina overheard him.

'Tell her . . . why you are wearing this shirt . . . tell her . . . why you chose blue only . . . '

Shivam looked embarrassed.

She lowered her gaze.

Shivam fumed. This singer would kill him with his well-intentioned ways. He dismissed him with a shove of his elbow, and started talking before Gulshan Kumar could drop in again to help.

Her eyes were cast down, staring at some invisible spot on the table.

'Look up,' he urged her.

'Why?'

But she lifted her gaze and looked right into him.

'Your eyes . . . ' he couldn't help but say.

'My eyes . . . ' she needed to hear it.

'They drown me with their depth, like blue waters.'

'And . . . ?'

'I'm obsessed with them. '

'Tell me something new,' she replied, her eyes dancing with mischief. 'Else . . . else, I'm going.'

'You can't,' he asserted. 'Not before you show me your full face.'

Her eyebrows rose in an unspoken question.

'Lift it . . . I want to see.'

'Here?' Her eyes opened wide in horror. 'Are you mad or what!'

'No one knows you here. Except me.'

'I can't.'

'A glimpse please,' he pleaded.

'Why should I? What do I get?' she played along.

'I'll tell you something you don't know.'

Her brows arched up in wonder.

'Shivam, *beta*!' Someone called out, freezing the boy's blood and forcing him to turn around.

It was Srivastav uncle, the neighbour who was always waxing eloquent about his son, Amulya. He had just entered the sweet shop and caught the boy sitting there alone.

'You are alone?' he asked, as he walked up to Shivam.

'I'm waiting for a friend,' Shivam said, recovering from the shock.

The man nodded.

'And you, uncle?' he repaid the courtesy by asking about him.

'I came to buy some sweets. Amulya has cleared his job interview na . . . that big Bangalore IT company, you know,' said the forty-five-year-old, chest swelling with pride.

Shivam nodded, waiting for the neighbour to finish his task and leave.

But life spins its own tale. Even as his Aaina sat waiting at the next table, Srivastav uncle droned on. 'Seems like yesterday, you two boys were playing cricket in the gali fighting over every run . . . and today,' his voice rose higher by a decibel, 'he's got a corporate job.'

Shivam nodded.

'You . . . you have not applied anywhere, have you? Still loitering around, I hear.' Then, without waiting for the response, he shook his head with regret, 'Mahantji must be a worried father. Don't do this to him. You are a grown-up young man. You need to help him out now.'

Shivam was beginning to get uncomfortable when the man's order arrived and he had to pay the bill. With his hands full of packets, he departed with a loud but distant goodbye.

Shivam returned to his Aaina, irritated at the interruption.

Her eyes were smiling, tickled by his exasperation. 'So, you *loiter*?' she said with a laugh.

'I chase my dream!' he said assertively.

'And that is . . . '

'First you show, then I'll tell.'

He was playing her game now. Teasing.

'I . . . I can't . . . '

Suddenly three boys entered the shop.

'Shivam Bhaiya!' one of them called out and the trio made their way to his table.

They were Shivam's juniors from college.

'Abbey, guys, what's up?'

'Bhaiya, you don't come to play now,' chimed one.

'A little busy these days. What's with you guys?'

'This tournament is on, Bhaiya . . . with the Govardhan colony,' one of them said excitedly. 'For the past three days, we are winning hundred rupees every day.'

'And you're blowing it on samosa only . . . or . . . ' Shivam implies alcohol.

'Arrey, Bhaiya, you know . . . even if it's Bisleri, full Ayodhya finds out.' The junior's pathetic expression had them all in splits.

The trio moved to a corner table and Shivam turned to Aaina's seat.

It was empty.

'Shit!' he swore under his breath. He walked over to where she was sitting . . . to breathe in the warmth of the space . . . He found a tissue folded and tucked under the tissue stand, bearing a message and a smiley on it. She had left it there for him. He picked it up, unfolded it and read it:

Saturday, 4 p.m. Mahila Mahavidyalaya lawn.

The boat glided past the Mahavidyalaya grounds. Before their boat docked at the ghat, the boys could see it stretching out beyond the verdant forest greens.

8

It would be evening soon. The Sarayu glinted golden as their boat bobbed up and down.

The boys were on a recce mission for the Saturday rendezvous. Their eyes scanned the school playground for an opening from where they could sneak in.

'Yaar, I can't see how we'll get in,' said Shivam sceptically.

'We'll figure something,' Babloo said confidently.

Shivam was still unsure.

'She's called us na this time . . . so she only has to get us in.'

'Us?' Shivam whacked his friend on his head. 'Don't forget she's your bhabhi!'

'Relax! I've got my music . . . there no place for girls in my life.'

'What if she can't?' Shivam returned to the issue.

'We'll stand gawking outside then . . . like before.'

'Yes, that we do best,' agreed Shivam, hugging his friend.

Babloo pushed him off. But Shivam slid up to him again, unable to contain his joy for tomorrow. They would find a way.

'Babloo, I feel like kissing you . . . you make me so happy.'

'You've got a girl. Still it's me you want to kiss!' said Babloo, jumping aside in disgust.

Shivam lunged to catch him. The boat rocked as the boys rolled over laughing. The mood changed.

Soon after, they docked the boat, tying it up before bouncing up the steps of the bathing ghat to their cycles, each pedalling onwards to his own destination.

* * *

There was a song in her step as she walked home that day. Her black-and-white world had suddenly gone technicolor for she has dared to reach out to life, listened to the flutter in her heart, and spent time with someone she wanted to spend time with, instead of hanging around for someone unknown to be thrust upon her as the right choice. All of this meant breaking the rules. And she had broken them, with a certain joy.

'You've got to follow the rules if you want to get anywhere in life,' Abbu was talking to someone over the phone—mouthing his life's dictum.

His words jolted the seventeen-year-old back into her jaded reality.

She hurried in, not wanting to dampen her mood and exuberance.

But there was Ammi to contend with. 'Salma's nikah has got fixed,' she informed her. 'It's coming Monday. Just one week to go. How will we manage!'

Aaina swallowed this. That explained why Abbu was home at this time of day. She looked around. It was as if some typhoon had struck their house this noon. The rectangular aluminium trunk box, which was stored under Ammi's bed, now cluttered the living room floor, its heavy concave lid thrown open and the contents spilling out. After sharing the good news, Ammi returned to the trunk. She sat on her haunches and went through the myriad ceremonial knick-knacks—embellished jugs and brass vase. Dry fruit packets lay on the sofa beside colourful velvet pouches in which they would be filled next. Naved was flitting in and out of the house, running errands for Abbu, while the older man conferred with the Imam and relatives on the nitty-gritty.

Salma was Aaina's cousin, her Mamu's daughter. Mamu was the only surviving brother Ammi had. All the arrangements for this nikah would have to be made at their house, Aaina knew.

'I want you to help sort the trunk with me first . . . then Naved's almirah . . . then . . . '

Abbu interrupted her. 'No more going to school now.'

'But Abbu . . . exams are close, I got . . . '

He cut her mid-sentence. 'You heard me. Till this nikah business is over, no going anywhere.'

Aaina looked from Abbu to Ammi. Ammi would understand but didn't have the courage to contradict him.

A full week to nikah. She would miss so many classes. And Shivam! How would she meet him on Saturday now? And how would she let him know she can't meet him. She felt trapped. *Life is about spreading your wings,* her mind screams. *And she will,* she promised herself with a determined shake of her head. *Yes,* I *will fly.*

'Don't daydream, there is lots to do,' Ammi prodded her.

Aaina joined her mother in emptying the trunk. Her hands did their task, her feet moved her along as she fetched, carried and placed stuff, and her ears listened to her Ammi's instructions but her mind remained lost. For someone lurked in it. Someone who watched her on the playground as she played . . . and when she made her way back home. Someone who . . .

'Fold those scarves properly!' Ammi snapped her out of her mental meandering.

Silk scarves, silver coins, sweets, jewellery, perfume, cosmetics . . . Abbu is listing out all the things that have to be arranged, after crossing out on the list what is already there.

Shivam had to go. It wouldn't do for him to clog her mind, when hundreds of nikah tasks loomed ahead. Aaina pushed out all that was exciting her and got busy with Mamu and Salma's things.

9

Noon, Tuesday, the December sun lessened the growing chill in the air somewhat. Shivam entered his courtyard, humming a soulful Sufi number and stepped on potato wafers laid out on sheets for sunning.

'Watch out!'

Ma left whatever she was grinding with her mortar-pestle and shuffled out from the kitchen to save her chips from her son, who was home for lunch.

But he kept goofing around with the half-dry, yellow slices. Balancing some on his head and a few more on his palms, he executed random dance moves, singing along happily.

His mother, however, was not amused. She pulled his ear and boxed it.

'You want to be a filmi hero now, do you?'

'Ma!' he shrieked and wriggled to free his ear.

Before she could shout at him, he pulled her into a tight hug.

Her anger dissipated in seconds. This boy of hers did everything wrong but knew the way to her heart.

Some mushy moments later, they disengage. 'Do you have to go again?' she asked him.

'Yes, Ma. Masterji told me to hurry back. This is peak time, he says. Orders for wedding clothes are coming in.'

His mother stopped herself from saying something disparaging. She made her way back to the kitchen, asking him to hurry and freshen up. 'I'll serve your lunch right away.'

But later, when she found him there and yet not there, she lost it. Sitting cross-legged, tearing a piece of the crisp, fluffy roti she had just made, he dipped it into the potato-pumpkin curry but instead of putting it in his mouth, he kept fiddling with it on the plate.

'What's wrong with you, Shivam?' she cried. 'You don't want to help Baba and now you don't want to eat also?' Food was an issue with her.

It made him snap back to the moment. Vignettes of the day before had been playing on his mind. At work, he had put a padlock on his thoughts. Murshid Mia, the master tailor and designer, was a hard taskmaster who expected his apprentice to give everything he had to master the craft. And Shivam did. Back home for lunch, he was free of work constraints and it had come gushing back. His heart broke into song and he broke into dance in the courtyard. Just one scene played on his mind now. The kitchen, the plate and the bite in hand, all of it receded into the background. Except her, everything was out-of-focus. He could see only Aaina—on the table next to him, looking at him, a bit excited, a bit nervous, but also playful, her words soothing him, her eyes bewitching him.

In the middle of this intoxicating memory, Ma started crying. She had been shouting at him earlier and he had ignored that. Her tears, he could not. So he blotted out every Aaina image flitting through his mind and slid up closer to his mother, dragging his steel plate alongside. With the back of his right hand, he wiped the tears off her cheeks.

'Shoo, now! Else I will be forced to rub my fingers sticky with food all over your face.'

The bluff worked. She dabbed her face dry with the free end of her saree and considered him morosely.

'Babuji called up,' she said, watching her son scoop a mouthful. 'Too much happening around the mandir today . . . more police has come.'

'Hmm . . . '

'Full place they have gheraoed . . . all are sitting in a ring.'

'Hmm . . . '

'What hmm?' She was annoyed again. 'Can't you go see him once? He is all alone there. Even some ministers have come.'

'Ma, Babuji is the head priest. No one can touch him. Relax.'

'How can you not worry,' she retorted. 'You are his flesh and blood.'

'Ma, with all that police out there guarding him . . . my going there will be useless.'

'You won't, then?'

'Arrey, ma, I will . . . I definitely will, if he needs me. But he does not. Not right now.'

'He needs you in the temple . . . you going there and doing what he has always done,' she argued.

'Now stop singing that old tune. I'm not going to be a priest. I'm telling you one final time, bas . . . I don't like it.'

'What do you like? Mussalmani work! . . . And those . . . those Mussalmani gaane that you keep singing!'

Shivam nodded, eating slowly, staring into his plate. He did not see the anger rising in his mother's eyes.

'I like . . . ' he said, looking vacant once more, 'blue eyes . . . the deepest blue . . . alluring . . . haunting blue.'

'You have gone mad.'

'Ma, you like blue eyes?'

'What?' This confounded her.

'Yes, blue,' he continued, lost again, 'like the sea . . . like an ocean . . . depths you can drown in.'

'Blue, blue . . . keep doing blue blue! Don't stitch that orange cut-piece Babuji gave you for Sita Ma. No, even the goddess doesn't matter to you now.'

'I will, Ma. I will,' he promised, getting up to keep his plate out for washing. 'But I got to rush now.'

He scrambles out of the kitchen after giving her a quick hug. She followed him out, asking him to be extra careful.

'The town is flooded with outsiders,' she warned him. 'Something bad is in the air.'

'Bad? I see no bad . . . only blue eyes.'

'Blue eyes?'

He pedalled away, leaving her confused and worried.

* * *

It was clear to Ammi that some djinn had gotten into her daughter. For she worked and yet not. Just four days to the wedding and things were getting maddening. The old woman had asked Aaina to gift-wrap clothes meant for the bridegroom's family and had handed the suits, gift boxes, ribbons and the wrapping paper to her. The girl had promptly completed the task, wrapping neatly, winding the shiny ribbon around each box, fashioning its golden ends into tiny bows that sat on the top, and stacking the colourful boxes neatly on the living room table. Only, as an aunt pointed out, Aaina had failed to fill the boxes! The clothes were still lying outside.

With relatives trickling in—some to visit and advise, others with bag and baggage and minds made up to stay until the nikah—Ammi somehow managed to find a quiet corner for a court martial with her daughter.

'Are you unwell?' she started on a polite note although she was seething.

'I don't know how the stuff came out,' Aaina replied. 'I am sure I had packed them.'

Ammi itched to whack her but too many eyes were on them and she didn't want a spectacle.

'Remember, we're doing all this for Mamu. And Salma is no less than you for me. There can be no mistake . . . in anything.' Ammi's eyes bored into her, brooking no argument . . . and no excuse.

Aaina could only nod in agreement.

'Now, will you go to the kitchen, make that rose sherbet and see that the drink is served to all the children?'

Aaina rushed off to do her bidding.

Naved, the ogre that he was, had been eavesdropping from behind the curtain.

He followed her into the kitchen and kept an eye on her as she went about her chores. He watched her mix the sherbet and pour it into glasses, which she then lined up on a tray. *But why was she smiling?*

Fortunately, Naved could not access what was in her head . . . for this head was stuck in Shivamland.

So he plays cricket . . . she said to herself, smiling. *And plays well. Those boys in the sweet shop said they missed him in the team. Well, he looked fit.*

'Will you move or keep standing here only.'

Aaina jumped, knocking down a glass of sherbet.

She had not seen Naved and his sudden comment startled her. She bent to pick up the shards of glass from the floor. A jagged edge cut her finger, making it bleed.

That sent Naved running to Ammi again.

Aaina was hunched on the kitchen floor, getting mad at the blood oozing down the side of her right palm. More than pain, she felt irritation. That idiot brother of hers would not be done bleating to Ammi only. He would escalate it to Abbu too.

She washed her hand and cleared up the mess, not waiting to call the maid. Minutes later, as she walked out with the tray, Ammi accosted her in the hall.

'Are you hurt?' she asked, taking the tray and calling out to a cousin to serve it around.

Before Aaina can answer, Ammi had lifted her hand to inspect it. There was a gash where the shard had grazed the skin and droplets still oozed crimson. Ammi took the girl into the room.

As she cleaned the wound with *Dettol* and fixed a Band-Aid on it, Ammi searched her daughter's face. 'What's wrong with you,' she asked. 'Tell me what's bothering you.'

'Nothing, Ammi . . . I . . . I was just thinking about what I could wear for the *walima* when this happened.'

Aaina knew Ammi would sense something else was up unless she gave her something legitimate.

'Ya Allah!' Ammi held her head. 'I forgot about your dresses totally in all this . . . come . . . come.'

Ammi nearly emptied out Aaina's cupboard on the bed. For the next twenty minutes, they mulled over which gharara she could wear for the mehndi ceremony, and whether a pink dupatta or the silver grey one would go well with the blue bismillah suit for the nikah.

'You are right,' declared Ammi, after rummaging through it all. 'You've got nothing for the walima.'

'It is okay, Ammi. I'll choose something out of all this.' Aaina did not want to bother her mother. She had brought up the dress only to avoid close questioning.

'No. You do need to get a kurta stitched. These won't do. Everyone will be looking at you.'

Aaina made a face. She did not want anyone looking at her. Except . . .

'Let me get those trunks put away first. Then . . . I'll take you.'

She tried convincing Ammi that she would manage with what she had but her mother was in no mood to listen. 'We'll go in a couple of hours, buy the fabric and give it for stitching.' Ammi left Aaina with a bed overflowing with her clothes and a nearly empty cupboard and just over an hour to put it all back together. There were too many aunts about the house for her to delaying this. She did not have the strength for another inquisition.

Although Aaina managed to rearrange her cupboard, clean up her room, and help make turmeric paste, Ammi was unable to go through the trunks. She was stuck with the jeweller; Abbu had called him to get the ornaments sorted, polished and checked.

'I can't go with you,' she told Aaina. 'All my fault, shouldn't have left your things for the last minute.'

'It's okay,' Aaina reassured her. 'I will manage.'

'Take Naved with you,' Ammi called out as she was about to leave. 'Too many ruffians are roaming the town these days.'

'No, Ammi.' Aaina rejected this option firmly. 'If he goes, I won't go.'

'But you can't go alone. Abbu will not agree.'

'I will ask Rehana to join me.'

Ammi sighed and nodded. Maybe her daughter was right—Naved could be a pain at times. She did not want her girl to come back half-way, abandoning all thoughts of getting a new kurta made.

Soon, Aaina was outside the noisy house, filled with relatives and vendors, and that nuisance of a Naved. She revelled in the joy of being by herself, after what seemed like an endless number of days. Out in the open, she breathed in lungfuls of the crisp, fresh December air and bounced along, enjoying her short walk. A rowdy group jostled past her, raising flags, singing raucously. Abbu had been right in cautioning Ammi. Never had she seen so many outsiders flock in here. Not even for *Ramnavmi*. There were policemen everywhere. Too much noise and movement . . . a carnival-like boisterousness was in the air. The town did not seem like her town today.

Aaina decided to hail a rickshaw for safety. She was on her way, unaware that the day would change the course of her life.

10

Even the most spacious tailoring shop in Ayodhya could get cramped at festival times. And in the hot and dusty north Indian towns, a significant drop in temperature was probably a bigger thing to celebrate than even the festivals on the calendar. Everyone wanted to flaunt new dresses and look their best with the changing season. The slight nip in the air had brought in a lot of business the master tailor's way.

The seventy-year-old asthmatic Masterji defied his age, gliding from one customer to another with the ease of a ballet dancer. He bent down to measure the lehenga length for Mrs Tiwari's daughter, handed over a finished package to another customer, squatted again to resume measurements, and lunged out to reach for the style book demanded by a new entrant. Mrs Tiwari could not help but praise his agility as she saw the old man rise to every demand without a sharp word or any show of irritation.

'Your attitude, Masterji . . . today's boys don't have it,' she gushed. 'No wonder everyone comes to you.' The old man blushed and shook his head.

More people trooped in and Mrs Tiwari had to make way for them.

While he was dealing with a fussy trio—who had ordered a batch of seven salwar kameezes they insisted had to be designer copies and kept flipping on which style they wanted on which fabric—a rickshaw pulled over and Aaina stepped out.

'Assalam Walekum, Chacha! Aaina Farooqui.'

'Walekum Assalam, beti,' he responded. The Farooqui family had been getting their clothes stitched by him for years.

'Chacha, it is Salma's nikah. I need to get a kurti stitched urgently.'

'When do you want it *beta*?' he asked, looking worried.

'On the fifth of this month Chacha,' she said nervously, looking at the crowd.

'Not possible,' he replied with a sigh, confirming her fears. 'There are too many orders already,' he said, looking around.

'But I never get it done from anyone else,' the girl pleaded.

'You should have come earlier, *mohtarma*,' the old man replied.

'Okay, sixth,' she bargained. 'I will pick by noon . . . by then you can surely manage.'

'Not possible before the twelfth,' Masterji declared, noting down the designs finally shortlisted by the picky trio.

'Chacha!' she was pleading now.

'Try to understand . . . it is already the third, how can it be done in three days?'

'I will do it.'

All heads turned to the voice emanating from somewhere inside the shop. Someone got up from behind the sewing machine at the back and came forward.

Aaina gasped. It was Shivam.

'Chacha?' Aaina turns to the old man, unsure about what Shivam was doing in the tailoring shop.

'He's my *shagird*,' smiled the old gentleman. 'He's training under me.'

'Oh!' She blushed a bit and looked down.

'I can make it,' repeated Shivam looking at her intently.

The old man was not so sure. 'This is a *nikah ki kurti*. You have not done this type before.'

'One learns by doing only na, as you say. I will learn.'

'It won't be easy . . . and in such short time.'

'I will work day and night on it . . . give it all I have . . . ' he stated, still looking at her.

'You will, I believe you, young man . . . but still I am not sure you should take it,' replied Masterji. 'There may be an issue . . . '

Aaina interrupted him, 'Let him do it, Chacha.'

The old man looked from one of them to the other. He was still not convinced. The number of orders he had was overwhelming. There was no way he could accommodate this too, on the off-chance something went wrong.

'You see,' he told them both. 'I will not take responsibility for this.'

'I won't let you down,' Shivam assured his mentor.

The old man motioned Aaina inside for the measurements. For a close-fitting nikah kurti, her six-month-old measurements wouldn't do.

The trio at the counter, watching the exchange with curiosity at first, was getting impatient. One of them drummed her fingers on the wooden counter top. Masterji turned his attention back to them.

Aaina entered the tiny curtained enclosure at the far end of the shop. Shivam followed her with a measuring tape slung around his shoulders, a tiny notepad and pen in his hands, and a heart that was beating at four times its normal speed.

'What you doing here?' she asked urgently in a whisper, the second he stepped in.

'What you are seeing me do now.'

'Darzi! Are you really a tailor?'

'Trying to be one,' he said, smiling. 'It is my passion.' He paused for a second and added, 'My second passion'.

She did not dare ask about his first passion.

Shivam came close, slid the tape off his shoulders and started measuring her. He began with the shoulders, holding the tape taut to note the distance between the shoulder blades on her back. He went on to the neckline, tracing its width at the back, slipped the tape down diagonally in the front then, stopping a few inches below the neck to know how deep she wanted the neckline to be.

'This much will do, or more,' he checked.

She didn't say anything.

'Aaina?'

'This is okay.' It took her a minute to confirm it. First, finding him here, then this nearness . . . Aaina was melting with shame.

He was conscious of their proximity too. Yet, he fought to sound normal and do his job. He wound the tape around her arm and reeled off a number that he jotted down on the pad.

Aaina watched him through her niqab. His touch, his words, even his breath affected her acutely.

'How long you want your sleeves to be?' Shivam asked. He ran his measuring tape down her shoulder, till it reached the elbow, and waited.

'Whatever you think is fine.' His fingers on her arm were clogging her thoughts.

Shivam looked up into her eyes then. He had been avoiding those oceans until now . . . scared of losing himself again in their depths. They looked even more alluring today—twin pools, shining blue and laughing at his confusion.

Getting bolder, he reached out to touch one of her cheeks over her niqab, making her shiver.

'Show me your face . . . ' he pleaded.

'Why should I?'

Her question threw him off. He peered into her eyes again for an answer. And got it. She was playing with him. The blue orbs were teasing him, dancing with mischief. Such a devil, she was! Her impish ways . . . that hint of wickedness . . . this had made him her slave.

'Okay, tell me, what should I do to see your face?'

Pat comes her answer. 'Beat me at kho-kho, that's what I want.'

'Kho-kho?'

'Yup. My friends said you cannot run . . . You only stand and stare,' she said with a laugh.

He resumed the measurement and laughed with her. Then he positioned the tape around her chest. Both held their breath as he noted down the measurement.

'Breathe normally,' he told her comfortingly while circling her waist with the tape, just above her belly button.

'So, you really know a lot about this,' she remarked, as the tape reached her hips. She was trying to dissipate the tension.

'Yes,' Shivam replied, standing straight again. 'Told you, it is my passion,' he locked eyes with her and continued, 'second to just you.'

She hit him playfully on his arm. And the tension was broken.

He held her hands in his and implored her again to lift her veil and let him see her.

'Okay, I will. But first you. . . '

'I will,' he cut her. 'I will beat you at kho-kho.'

'No, you can't,' she shook her covered head fiercely. Suddenly, she remembered something. 'Oh and I can't come on Saturday now. Abbu has stopped all outings till my cousin Salma's nikah.'

'Stopped all outings?' Shivam repeated it as a question. 'But you will have to come for your final kurti fitting?' He looked disheartened.

'Okay, I will sneak out, somehow,' she told him, aghast at his fallen face. 'And . . . '

'Shivam!' Masterji called out from the counter.

She let go of his hands and hurried out of the curtained enclosure, with a promise. 'And you can see my face too . . . if . . . if your kurti fits me just the way I want it to.'

'It will,' he promised.

He followed her out, picking up his tape, pen and notebook from the stool inside.

There are no more customers at the shop now.

'You told him how you want it?' Murshid Mia checked with Aaina as she was about to leave. She nodded.

'Yes, he is a bright boy.'

Aaina nodded and was almost out of the shop when the senior tailor called out, 'Aaina beti, did you give the fabric? Where is it?'

Aaina turned around to look at Shivam. She had forgotten all about it! Ammi had told her to buy the fabric on her way.

Shivam had occupied so much space in her head lately that every other thing had slipped away. Annoyed with herself, Aaina held her head and cursed herself.

'She gave it to me,' Shivam told Masterji. 'It is fine, I've seen.'

Masterji nodded and moved on to other things.

Aaina looked from the one to the other . . . not having understood what had happened. Shivam tilted his head sideways, ever so slightly, telling her he would take care of it. She looked at him, and knew that he would. Her smile reached her eyes.

11

Rehana, Seema and Meher were talking all at once, above the commotion that filled a house bursting with relatives. Aaina gave up trying to figure what anyone was saying.

'Find a quiet corner na,' shouted Rehana into her friend's ear.

'Don't burst my eardrum,' cried Aaina, drawing away.

Ammi overheard this and felt sorry for her daughter. The girl had been her right hand through the preparations, staying up from sunrise to late nights, at the beck and call of not just her Ammi but also the five aunts who were staying with them. She had never seen this side of her daughter. Though lost at times, forgetting where she'd kept something or who she'd carried the message for, Aaina had run from room to room, up the terrace too, fulfilling everyone's wishes. She deserved a break.

'Go out with them for some time,' Ammi whispered in her daughter's ear, allowing her to spend some time with her friends. This made her squeal with joy.

The very next minute, she pranced out to the street with her friends, thrilled to breathe in the open air.

Rehana laughed, watching Aaina skip. 'You act like you been locked up since ages!'

'Forty hours madam . . . and how slowly each hour has passed.' Aaina struck a dramatic pose like a Hindi film heroine as she spoke and the group doubled up with laughter.

At a street side stall, as they waited to be served the tangy, spicy chaat, Aaina told them about her encounter in the tailor's shop. 'So movie-like . . . ' drooled Meher.

'Lucky you! I've never found anyone, no matter where I go,' lamented Rehana. 'Be it tailor or grocer.'

Seema added, 'I feel worse. I don't even have a burqa, still, no boy climbs a water tank to stare at me.'

This sent all four tittering again.

'Saturday,' recalled Meher. 'You were to meet him on Saturday, na?'

Before Aaina could open her mouth, Seema interrupted, 'The nikah is tomorrow. How can she leave?'

'Exactly!' agreed Meher. 'But what about now? . . . Who's stopping her?' She raises her brow.

The four girls looked at each other and were suddenly excited. Minutes later, the idea took the shape of a plan. Rehana dialled Babloo's sister from a shop. She knew Babita didi. Through her, she sent a message to Babloo and his friend.

'Tell them we are playing kho-kho on the grounds behind the Company Bagh.' Before the shopkeeper could suspect anything, Rehana disconnected the line and walked out.

'Done,' she informed the trio waiting outside, rubbing her hands in glee.

'Now, we'll see how strong her love is. And how deep.'

'Yup, we will know today. Maybe, it's just a passing fancy.'

The girls ribbed their friend even as they hurried to Company Bagh. There was not much time. Aaina would have to return home soon. She hurried along with them, both nervous and excited.

Fifteen minutes later, as the girls poured out of their rickshaws, they found the boys already waiting outside the gates.

'Wah!' Meher let out. 'Your hero beats the movie-wallah hero.'

'Arrey, this hero is unemployed, so totally free.' It was Seema now. The three girls went on like this, giggling as they ushered their friend in.

Behind the girls, the boys entered the empty grounds adjacent to the famous Company Bagh.

'Here, I am,' Shivam announced to his girl, once they were inside.

'I can see that,' she replied. 'Say something I don't know.'

'I can say a hundred things but your eyes . . . ' Shivam stopped to gaze into them, 'your eyes make me lose my mind . . . my voice . . . everything!'

'Watch it!' Rehana cautioned her friend playfully. 'It is only that blue colour he is after.'

'My kurti . . . how is it shaping up?' Aaina asked, changing the topic.

'You see for yourself on the sixth.'

'Why don't you show him your face,' Babloo butted in. 'That will fire him to work better.'

'I will . . . if he can catch me,' replied Aaina, taking off her sandals.

Shivam and Babloo looked puzzled as the girls sat down in position for a game of kho-kho. Aaina stood waiting at one end of the file.

'Catch me,' called out Aaina.

'What's this Bhaiya . . . are they mad!'

Deaf to his friend, Shivam threw off his sandals and began chasing Aaina, both running barefoot on the grassy grounds. But she was too fast. Even with the burqa billowing behind her in the December breeze, she stayed a foot and a half ahead of him all the time.

Shivam was fit and raced with all his might. He came within touching distance of the flying end of her black robe . . . but that was about it. She scampered ahead before he could close the gap.

By the fourth round, Shivam was panting and gave up. He dropped down on the grass, breathing heavily while Aaina now stood laughing with her group.

This got to Babloo. 'This is unfair,' he pronounced. 'You challenged Bhaiya in your game. Not his.'

But before anyone could say anything, Rehana pointed out that it was getting late and that Aaina needed to be home.

'See your own face now. Loser,' she mocked him, on her way out of the grounds.

'You won't get your kurti until you show your face,' he countered.

'One defect,' she said, in her rush to go out, 'if I see one defect, I won't show you even my toe.'

'Done!'

With that, Shivam bounced up from the grass, brushed off the dirt clinging to his pants and walked out with an arm flung around Babloo's shoulders. They could hear the girls giggling as they boarded their rickshaws.

'Bhaiya, will you be able to manage the kurti?'

Shivam did not reply. Babloo got on a bicycle beside him.

'That's your only chance, Bhaiya. Otherwise she won't budge.'

Shivam pedalled on silently, with Babloo a bit behind him.

'Now where are we going?' Babloo asked as Shivam took a different turn.

'Murshid Mia's.'

'Murshid Mia's? Now?' Babloo pedalled furiously after his friend, who had taken the evening off from the old man.

'Till I don't finish the kurti, that's where I shall be,' said Shivam.

'Sew up your brains also, Bhaiya. You seem to be losing them,' said Babloo.

All Shivam could see was Aaina, hiding behind his mother as he chased her around their courtyard. He smiled. One day . . .

12

Like she had forgotten to get the fabric, Aaina had also failed
to tell him what sort of bottom she wanted for her kurti.
A churidar would have been the easiest. But every other girl
at the gathering would be wearing similar fitted pyjamas. So
Shivam rejected the idea outright. He explored more exotic
options. All of Wednesday, he sat yo-yoing between a sharara
and a gharara. These flared pants from the Mughal times had
become trendy; Hindi film heroines were dancing in them in
recent blockbusters. He was in a dilemma. *His girl would rock
in either.*

Wide-legged and flaring, the sharara oozed class and
a bygone era. He could see her sashaying around in them,
graceful and seductive. *But that minx in her . . . would it not get
stifled in all that show of elegance.* Shivam nodded at this new
thought. *Something sassy, she needs. A gharara then. Tight-fitted
and ruched at the knees, only to flare out dramatically under, this was
more in tune with her personality. Paired with a body hugging kurti
that steals every single heart in the walima hall. No, that she was not
allowed to do. She was destined only for one heart—his.*

With his mind made up, he started working on the
gharara suit. He pored over his draft—imagining her as he cut

the pattern. *She is here with him, wagging those thin painted fingers—with a take on everything he does, always ahead of him. Wanting him to play catch-up. She-devil, Aaina is! His own sprite. How he loves this wickedness in her! Maybe even more than her eyes.* Shivam sighed. *She unsettles him so . . . he will breathe once he sees her . . .*

He gives her kurti a sweetheart neckline, accentuating the décolletage, knowing it will make her neck seem longer. He has not seen her neck but knows it must be slender and delicate.

He had told her he would arrange for the fabric. It struck him that fate had arranged for it already—that radiant orange piece Babuji had given him to stitch . . . for the goddess. It would make for a stunning kurti. Flamboyant in colour, with tone-on-tone embroidery. His Aaina would glow in it. Like a goddess! For the gharara bottom, he would need to buy plain silk. But how? Where would he get the money from? He was just an apprentice, yet to start earning. And Babuji would ask him a hundred questions before parting with anything more than a hundred rupees. Shivam was still pondering on it as he wounded up work and walked up to unlock his cycle. But instead of mounting it he stood watching it. *Cycle! That's it.* He smiled, having figured how to buy the silk for her gharara.

* * *

So many purchases were still pending. Besides suits, jewellery and gifts, a nikah calls for a stocking up of umpteen other things, all equally important. Ammi's brother, being a heart patient, had put Abbu in charge of the arrangements. Abbu, an official in the state government, had called up the many contacts he had across businesses and government departments, looking for assistance. They would help him buy items at wholesale rates, he believed. His contacts proved useful, but in a totally different way. They warned him that things had changed rapidly in the past few days.

'Keep it simple and short,' said one.

'Hold the events in-house or shift them to Faizabad,' advised another.

'Postpone it. This is not the right time for it,' suggested a key officer in the Culture Department.

Half the arrangements had already been made. It was only in these past three days that this new uncertainty had gripped the town, raising many doubts in the local minds. Mr Farooqui got anxious. So many outsiders had flooded Ayodhya overnight. Hundreds were camping in tents near the disputed religious site.

'Rates for everything have doubled,' reported the man Abbu had sent out to buy groceries and rent bedding, blankets and plastic chairs because more guests were expected two days before the nikah. The fellow had returned with not even half the stuff Abbu had listed. The sudden deluge of visitors had upped the demand for basic things, the price of essentials had hit the roof. All this hit Abbu hard.

And it was not just the prices. The air was thick with rumours and a sense of uncertainty that made it difficult to plan or even book services such as that of the florist, decorator, caterer and photographer. The make-up artist Salma had booked from Lucknow had called to cancel. Even the local girl Ammi had summoned to apply mehndi for the bride and all the other women had refused to come.

'What should I do?' Abbu spoke to Mr Ansari then, calling up his Lucknow friend, whose nephew was an inspector in the city's police department.

'It's not a good time for the community . . . especially in Ayodhya,' his friend cautioned.

Abbu turned to Mamu to discuss this. 'Should we cancel the walima and have just the nikah?'

'What about the advance we have given for the hall?' Mamu pointed out. 'They won't refund.' The father of the bride was worried about the finances too.

There was no getting around the problem. Abbu decided to take his chances and go ahead with the programme as planned. Only now the celebrations would be more muted.

Though Aaina, doing Ammi's bidding, walked in and out of the living room several times while the discussion was on, she registered nothing about the conversation or the tension in the air. Her mind was full of other things . . . delicious things . . . things that refused to make space for anything else.

* * *

Too much was going on at Shivam's place too, with all kinds of people landing up at their doorstep—politicians, religious leaders, influential local heads. Much talk was on . . . in hushed voices, which often rose to argue . . . and fell again when someone in the group reminded them to keep things low. Mahantji was found more at home, discussing important things, than worshipping at the Hanuman temple he was in charge of. He did go there to conduct the daily rituals, but that was it. He no longer lingered to attend to devotees or supervise the cleaning up after the pujas and prasad-offering to the deity. There was a stream of people to meet him these days. They came for his support and advice, or so they said.

It was almost midnight when Shivam steered the bicycle he had borrowed from Babloo to a stop outside his house. His own bicycle was Rajan's now, sold to fund the silk for the gharara bottom. He found that the spot he parked his cycle was occupied by two Ambassador cars, both with red beacons, announcing the exalted status of the passengers they'd carried to his front door. A Maruti car, two scooters and a police jeep were also parked alongside. Men in uniform were hanging around, on escort duty.

Babloo was right, things were worse than he thought them to be. Brushing past the security personnel, Shivam tried to enter, dragging his cycle inside with him. But he was stopped.

What the hell! . . . They won't let me enter my own house or what?

Shivam raised his voice, 'Yaar, I can stop your entry here . . . you can't.'

His mother heard the commotion and rushed out. She calmed all of them and took her son in.

'Too many important people inside,' she told him in a whisper. 'Mind your ways.'

'Important!' Shivam smirked as he leaned his cycle against the inner courtyard wall. 'All they care about is power . . . and their own pockets.'

His mother shushed him with an angry look. She showed him that they were all in Babuji's room and cautioned him that his voice would carry to them.

Shivam shook his head and ran up to his room. He wanted no role in all this religious drama. He had worked, without blinking, to finish Aaina's nikah outfit. Only the hooks and lace edgings remained to be sewn in. He had started early in the day because there were other orders Masterji had passed to him. Around midnight, Murshid Mia had thrown him out of the shop, insisting he had to lock the place and go. Masterji was as impressed by his apprentice's devotion as with his talent. The old man was unaware of the love angle behind this extra-human effort being put into the kurti.

Babloo scampered up to Shivam's room just as he had finished changing and was about to hit the bed and catch a few winks before dawn broke on the D-day. *Yes, it would mark an important turning point in his life. She would show him her face. And together they would begin their journey on the path they have chosen to carve out for themselves. Yes, tomorrow! He would start the day by doing the hooks.*

'Bhaiya!' Babloo shook his friend back to reality. He shoved a steel plate laden with roti and vegetables into Shivam's face.

'Mausi has told you to eat up here only. Too many bigwigs are loitering downstairs.'

The sight of his friend up here at this hour startled Shivam.

'You want money for some new cassette?' he asked.

'No, I want nothing,' He said quickly. 'I manage my own cash most of the times, *Bhaiya* . . . only, sometimes, I come to you.' He sounded hurt.

'Oye, overacting *ki dukaan*! Here, have this paneer curry, it's amazing . . . and stop whining.'

As the boys feasted on the curry and roti, Babloo confided in him about how the tension in the town was getting to him.

'Everyone's saying just one thing . . . something's going to happen . . . something big is going to happen . . . '

Shivam nodded and rose to wash his hands.

'And Bhaiya,' Babloo continued, his eyes large with fear, 'they are terrified . . . yes, everyone's terrified.' His voice dropped to a whisper as he said this. Clearly, the boy was as rattled as the town with the recent goings-on. That was the reason he had come to his friend at this late hour. 'Bhaiya, can I stay here with you tonight?'

Shivam found this amusing and burst out laughing. For the next fifteen minutes, he teased his musical friend on how he ought to pawn his lousy voice to invest in some muscle and power. This was precisely what Babloo needed at this hour to change his mood.

After all this goofing around, the two lay on their backs, talking about things.

'Bhaiya, listen to this cassette na, it's like your heart is talking to you.'

'Why your heart never talks to you, Babloo?'

The question had sprung up from nowhere but now that Shivam thought of it, it was strange that his friend had never expressed an opinion or interest in any girl. *Was he?* He turned to look at the young man lying next to him, dressed in kurta jeans. He had already plugged in the song on his small Walkman and was shaking his head with the music. Shivam sighed and listened in.

13

Morning dawned. Shivam had barely slept. During the little sleep that he got, he was dreaming. Up with the sun, he ran out. To the Sarayu. Wanting to dive in. And pray to the river for blessings. The Sarayu was an intrinsic part of his life.

He heard the temple bells toll as the gods are woken up lovingly and venerated. Shivam folded his hands in front of a deity, offered some flowers and took his cycle to the sabzi mandi, the vegetable market. A song from a faraway radio lifted his heart as he pedalled rhythmically. He reached his destination in a matter of minutes. This particularly congested area of Ayodhya was quiet and forlorn at that hour. But for some reason, a special police contingent was stationed at the roundabout that day. The men, sitting or standing, were half-awake although on. The litter strewn across the lane greeted him as he made his way towards Murshid Mia's shop.

He was early. Those days, even Masterji came to work hours before the shop officially opened. He was swamped with orders and wanted to finish as much work as he could in the early morning hours when he would not be disturbed. But not at 6 a.m. No, unlike Shivam, Masterji was not driven by love or hormones to land there at dawn.

The head priest's son wandered around a bit, waiting for the old man to appear and for his day to officially begin. Someone who was cycling by stopped next to him. It was the newspaper boy. He had finished his rounds and, sighting a familiar face, paused to chitchat.

'Shivam Bhaiya, you here, at this hour?'

'Work,' Shivam told him.

'Kya Bhaiya, don't tell me you too are cursed like me . . . working such odd hours.'

Shivam smiled, pulled out a Hindi paper from the stack peeping out of the fellow's sling bag, and began to read:

6 December 1992: Hundreds of right-wing activists have congregated at the historic town of Ayodhya after their Rath Yatra to garner support for a temple at the disputed site. The state government has rushed additional police forces to the town and cordoned off the sensitive areas. But the town is like a tinderbox, one spark could inflame passions and char lives.

The newspaper hawker interrupted him, 'We've never had these fights here before. This Hindu–Muslim thing . . . have we?'

Shivam nodded. None he could recall.

'It's these bloody outsiders, all this ruckus is their doing!'

'Yes, and we have to pay,' replied Shivam.

A policeman shouted from behind them, rapped the newspaper wallah for standing in the middle of the lane and chatting.

The boy pedalled away, muttering that the bloody police was acting like this was Kashmir and they were under curfew.

Shivam panicked, realizing that things were far more serious than he had presumed. He had been blind and deaf to the goings on. *Babloo was right. Things are actually bad! There is unease in the air. Like they are all waiting for something. They want to stop it . . . but don't know what exactly to stop, and how. The ring of security in the town should make him feel safe. But why was he feeling different?* Shivam shivered at his thoughts.

Murshid Mia arrived on his scooter soon after and they opened the shop. As Shivam measured out the zari he needed to stitch on the kurti, all thoughts of the local situation evaporated. Only Aaina and her kurti ruled his mind.

It did not take him more than an hour to finish the lace and hooks. His labour of love was ready. Now he only had to wait for his love to arrive and make it hers. He took the kurti to Masterji and spread it before him for his opinion. Murshid Mia was impressed, not just with the cut and styling but also with his neat work. He passed another two dress orders, which required careful and intricate work, to Shivam. This promotion would have given Shivam a high on any other day except today. As the hours went by, he was finding it more and more difficult to concentrate on his work, or on anything else. Every few minutes, he would turn his wrist to check the time. 9 a.m. . . 10 . . . 11 . . . and 12.15 now. *She couldn't have forgotten. No. Then why is she making him wait this way? Teasing him, was she? It's possible. With her, anything was possible. But wasn't this part of her charm!* Shivam smiled at the thought.

Masterji turned to show him something and was tickled to see the boy smiling at nothing. But before he could quiz him on it, he had some visitors. No, they were not customers. Three men—two of them middle-aged and one quite old—had trooped into the shop. They came past the front counter and drew Masterji into a huddle, inside the curtained trial room. They conferred in whispers that Shivam could not help but overhear as he was sitting by the nearby sewing machine.

'Thousands . . . thousands are there in those tents . . . most of them armed.'

'All this police force that's come,' Masterji intervened, 'they will take care.'

'Don't be naïve,' shouted one of them. 'They're with them . . . even they want a temple.'

'I've seen them chatting . . . even eating with those ruffians in the tents . . . supplying them stuff,' added another.

'What should we do then?' Masterji's his voice was really low now, his confidence shaken.

'Be wary. And run. At the first sign of trouble . . . run.'

'Low . . . speak low,' admonished someone. 'That Hindu boy is sitting just outside.'

And the voices dropped. Shivam could still hear them if he wished but he wanted none of this. He walked out of the shop for some air. He stood just outside the front counter and waited for the meeting to end. *No, he would not stray far, he could not afford to. She might come any moment now. In fact, she might already be there.* And that one thought was enough to drive away any tension that may have lurked in him after overhearing that talk inside.

The visitors soon left because a couple of customers came asking for Masterji. Shivam regained his perch at the work table inside, while Masterji attended to them.

Another hour rolled by. Shivam sat drumming his fingers on the table more than working. *Isn't the function in the evening? Why isn't she here till now? Had they barred her from stepping out?*

Everyone seemed to be blowing up the situation, making things seem far worse than they were.

Shivam stomped his foot in anger and disgust. Masterji jumped at the noise and turned to look at him. He was on edge too. Ever since that meeting in the trial room, his usual poised demeanour was gone.

'Something bit me.' Embarrassed at his sudden outburst, Shivam made an excuse.

Nodding, Murshid Mia went back to stacking orders for delivery. He wanted to wind up things a bit early and close shop by evening to be on the safe side. But there were a few important trials and deliveries lined up for the day. These were for regular customers and he would have to wait until they showed up.

Shivam picked up a lehenga panel and pretended to work on it, his mind galaxies away from the pieces of fabric on his table.

'Assalam Walekum, Chacha!'

His head jerked up at that voice, the lehenga panel slid to the floor.

'Walekum Assalam, beti,' greeted Masterji.

'You've come alone . . . ' Masterji observed in a disapproving tone 'not a good time to be out and . . . '

Shivam jumped in to cut him, 'It's her fitting and delivery . . . for that nikah kurti . . . she had to come.'

'You should've sent someone to collect.' The old man was not convinced that it was a good idea for her to show up. 'But now that you're here, come in,' he said and motioned her towards the trial room, where Shivam now stood, holding her outfit. 'Let's free you fast so you can go,' said Masterji, almost as an instruction to Shivam, who nodded in understanding.

Aaina took the suit from Shivam and stepped behind the tiny, curtained room.

While she was getting into her new outfit, Shivam and Masterji waited at the front counter, their back to the trial room.

'Murshid Mia!' A middle-aged man in kurta pyjama called out even as they heard the sound of his feet before he reached the shop. Masterji hurried out to meet him. Shivam saw the duo cross over to the other side and talk, their heads bent close together. Just then a group sauntered past, singing lustily, raising flags and sloganeering. He immediately peeked at the police personnel he had seen in the morning. They were standing in a group in the far corner, and gawking. He had watched them march up and down the lane, in twos and threes, at regular intervals. It was surprising they weren't saying anything now. However, at this time, Shivam's eyes were on the road but his mind was on the girl inside.

'Shivam!' Masterji called him. The boy ran up to his mentor, praying Aaina would not reach out to him that very instant. 'Can you mind the shop for seven-eight minutes,' requested the old man. 'I have to go up to the next lane for some urgent work. I'll see to it and rush back.'

'Yes, I'll manage,' Shivam replied. This seemed like a God-sent opportunity to be alone with his Aaina. He sprinted back to the shop, pushing his way past another rowdy group passing by.

'Watch it . . . ass . . .' threatened one of them, as he hemmed past them. Shivam ignored them and returned to Aaina. Nothing else mattered to him.

Murshid Mia hobbled on, going as fast as his legs could carry him. Unknown to Shivam, the man who walked away with Murshid Mia was his cousin, who had come to warn him that the gathered hooligans had just beaten up journalists waiting outside the Manas Bhawan guest house. The police, the huge state contingent posted there and at the Masjid site, had stood there like mute spectators, not protecting anyone who was attacked. 'They'll be coming for us next,' the cousin confided. 'I heard them raise slogans against us,' he said as he went to meet one of their community leaders, who had his office nearby. They would ask for temporary shelter with him before shifting with their family to neighbouring Faizabad.

As the clamour for the temple got insistent, forcing everyone around to get moving, Shivam sat waiting. His world, unlike that of the rest, revolved around an axis called Aaina.

14

'**S**hivaaaam!'

It seemed like he had been waiting for it forever and finally . . . finally, she'd called out to him.

Running his fingers through his hair nervously, the twenty-one-year-old stood outside, waiting for the curtain to be drawn, tingling with excitement.

And there she was, holding the curtain back, her burqa lying on a stool. She was still wearing the veil covering her face till the shoulders. She was standing so close to him that he went numb for a minute. He had been waiting for this moment for months and now when she was before him, he couldn't believe it was happening, that he was actually looking at her, radiant in his work, an alluring vision in orange, so perfectly proportioned, a poem in flesh and blood. She seemed nervous herself, fiddling with her dupatta, her slim fingers with silver nail polish going around it in knots.

He was seeing her without her burqa for the first time and she was far prettier than he had imagined. He saw her slender legs snug in the gharara, her slim figure fitting perfectly into the kurti, with her long dark-brown hair down to her waist. *If only she would turn around and he could see the exact length of her hair. But then he would want to touch it. It was better that she didn't turn around.*

He had been holding his breath for too long and now became completely tongue-tied.

She was braver than him and broke the silence. 'Am I looking fine?'

He kept looking at her, fighting to find words.

'Is it okay from the back,' she asked and twirled around for him to see.

Such a witch, she was! She knew he was now putty in her hands and how she was enjoying it. Well, he would show her that two can play this game.

So he stepped closer, within breathing distance, and reached out to check the fitting at the waist. His hands moved up a few inches, pinching the side seam to check if it ballooned out at points and needed a tuck.

Now, it was Aaina who could not breathe, trapped in her own seduction game.

'Perfect!' he pronounced finally, looking into her eyes.

She looked down shyly. She was getting self-conscious and broke eye contact.

'My kurti's perfect,' said Shivam, teasing her.

'And me?' The words were out before her mind could think it through and control what she was saying.

Shivam took a few steps back and tilted his head, acting like he was sizing her up before he could answer her.

Her eyes darkened in anger, 'Kurti . . . kurti . . . kurti! You're obsessed with your kurti.'

'No.' Drawing close to her once again, he told her softly, 'You know who I'm obsessed with.'

'All talk . . .' She shook her head.

He pulled her hard to him and held her tight, right next to his beating heart.

'Listen to this,' he whispered to her and put her hand on his chest.

Thud thud thud. It was his heart, beating at twice, thrice, maybe ten times the normal rate. She heard its thud, as loud and fast as her own, out of control. Minutes passed. They stayed like that, mindful of nothing and no one, except each other.

The ruckus outside seeped through the curtains but did not reach their ears.

'Show me,' demanded Shivam, hating the net and fabric niqab separating them.

'Lift it,' she ordered. 'Why should I do all the work?'

The minx! Shivam threw back his head and laughed.

It was this laugh that saved them. Babloo heard him and jumped into the shop, brushing aside the curtains of the trial room.

'Bhaiya!' he cried out. 'Thank God, I found you!'

Shivam swung around, the panic in Babloo's voice was searing. Aaina managed to disentangle herself from the embrace just in time.

'They've . . . Bhaiya, they've demolished the masjid!'

'What?'

Shivam froze. So did Aaina. They had not seen this coming. No one had. *There was tension, yes . . . but this . . . this was too much . . . too horrific . . . Hell! All hell would break loose now.*

'Bhaiya, Mahantji is in danger,' Babloo shrieked. 'You got to go . . . the Muslims, they . . . ' Babloo paused, considering Aaina's presence, 'they won't spare him, everyone's saying . . . '

A scream rent the air, drowning out the rest of his speech. There was a loud clanging of metal as something came crashing down. All three rushed up to the shop front, Shivam holding Aaina's hand.

Vandals had taken over the streets. In hordes, they roamed about, swinging clubs and swords, chanting, pillaging. Shivam saw them loot Akram Mia's shop and shatter the glassware on display with impunity and a recklessness that showed complete disregard for the law and the authorities. Most of the shutters were already down, the shopkeepers having fled or joined the mayhem. A group in skullcaps came around, pelting stones, ready to confront the other groups. Passers-by caught in the violence screamed and ran.

'Back gate! There is a back gate!' Shivam informed the other two, rummaging the drawers in the side almirah for the key. 'Babloo, clear the machines from there, fast.'

'We won't make it,' Babloo snivelled, even as he pushed the sewing machines away from the locked door to the far wall.

The commotion outside had only become louder. Shivam found the key and sprinted up to the tiny back entrance and unlocked it, his fingers trembling in fear.

'Wait,' he told Babloo, who was right behind him as he craned his neck to check the back lane before they hurtled out. It looked deserted. There was some pattering of feet as the odd person ran past this narrow alley, through which ran an open drain line. The three of them jumped out. Just in time. For minutes later, the shop was plundered, and everything in it, including the machines, was broken.

'Bhaiya,' gasped Babloo, as they raced down the alley, Shivam holding Aaina's hand tight. 'Bhaiya, you go to Mahantji. I'll take her home.'

Shivam was torn. He couldn't let her go, yet he couldn't go with her. Not when his father and his mother needed him. Just then Aaina shook off her hand, deciding for him. She looked into his eyes, urging him to leave.

'Babloo,' his voice quivering, Shivam spelled it out, 'you know she is my life.'

Babloo nodded. Shivam fished out a silver trinket from his pocket and fastened it around Aaina's wrist. A charm bracelet. He had bought it from what was left after he sold off his cycle to buy the silk for her gharara.

And then, they were gone. Shivam took a deep breath and headed in the opposite direction.

15

That was the last time he saw her.

Again and again, he goes down that road strewn with memories . . . some happy, some painful—all indelible. Its ten years today. Ten years since he laid his eyes on this kurti.

It is past midnight but Shivam is reluctant to let go of the orange dress the driver of the silver Honda City brought to his shop for alteration. *Alter!* Shivam laughs at the irony. The dress has altered the course of his life . . . and it is doing the same thing yet again, today, ten years later.

Soft, seductive and mysterious, flirting with her eyes and her words, in the way she moved, turned and giggled . . . she had killed him in this very kurti. Even with her niqab on. He smiles, remembering her earrings, silver circles that peeped through the veil every time she nodded. He keeps smiling even as sleep overcomes him. In the depths of slumber, the colours change. Orange turns black. Dark and deadly. In place of the kurti is a burqa . . . the charred remains of a burqa.

Shivam gets up with a start. Sweating. Breathing hard. The darkness of the night pales before the shadow inside him . . . the shadow of death . . . a final parting . . .

It had been a hurried goodbye in the alley that day. The . . . date was blotted in the calendars of history . . . as the domes came down. One God was robbed of his abode to make space for another God, or so everyone believed. Shivam was worse off . . . he had been robbed of his life, the reason for his existence. He remembers what Babloo recounted.

His friend had not let him down. Babloo had taken Aaina past the hooligans and the God's keepers, escorting her safely to her home in the Muslim-dominated part of Ayodhya–Qaziana. He had managed to get her through the town roiling with riots, where everyone seemed to be baying for each other's blood.

As he turned to go home, he fell down. A boisterous group out to attack Qaziana residents trampled over him and injured his ankle.

The air was rent with cries . . . cries of faith . . . of revenge . . . of terror. Babloo could do nothing but watch from where he lay on the street, holding on to his bruised leg, too petrified to move a muscle. Men, women and children poured out of the houses—some in kurtas, skullcaps or burqas, others having abandoned their traditional costume for fear of being marked out. They ran down the lane, screaming, praying, clutching on to their little ones and whatever else they had decided to carry with them. The rioters torched the houses. They even torched vehicles as some of them tried to flee in them. Babloo turned to stone, there was nothing he could do but watch.

Then he saw Aaina and her family scramble out of their house, the old mansion where he had left her. Fourteen-fifteen of them spilled out, her parents, brother, aunts and uncles and children. Many ran out in their billowy burqas and squeezed into the two cars waiting outside their door. He saw her get in too and heaved a sigh of relief. But he had been too soon to thank God. Within minutes, the goons surrounded the vehicles, forcing them to brake. They brought down their rods, smashing windshields and window glass. As the passengers struggled to jump out, someone chucked burning rags and set the cars ablaze.

The cars burned on. But those inside stopped struggling . . . they stopped crying. The flames had snuffed out their lives . . . the smoke turned them invisible. The attackers marched away, feeling victorious.

In a matter of minutes, it was all over. Babloo could see no more. The place emptied out soon. Those who would have mourned the dead had chosen to escape.

Leaning on the frame of a damaged hand cart, Babloo got up and hobbled off.

'*Jai Shri Ram,*' chanted Shivam, joining the supporters in their march to set things right. This was the only way he could reach the main temple safely and quickly. That's where Babuji was, with his newfound political and activist cohorts. Also, Ma was pottering about in their house in the temple complex, waiting for him.

The next day, Shivam's eyes welled with tears as he remembered what had unfolded the previous day.

'Don't,' admonished a sadhu in loose robes and painted forehead, his hair knotted in a tail. He reached out to Shivam, who was in the seat next to him on the UP Roadways bus driving out of Ayodhya in the early hours, before the curfew started. 'It's a day to rejoice,' he continued. 'Whatever you left behind doesn't matter. God got his space.'

Shivam rose and changed his seat to another in the front. He needed to be away from everything and everyone.

His eyes closed, mind and heart bleeding with memories, the boy had left the town that had been home to him from when he had first opened his eyes in this world. *Yes, he was leaving. But was there anything left to leave?* He opened the newspaper in his hand to look again at the picture tucked in one corner of the local daily, of a thick-set man with a broad nose and a severe visage. The headline said:

Head Priest of the Hanuman Temple Beaten to Death
Rioters had not spared the priest's wife either. They had killed her in cold blood.

His tears stained the paper. Shivam had not been with them when they needed him the most. Ma had told him time and again, Babuji needed him in the temple. He had not taken her seriously, insisting he did not want to be a priest. Babuji was an important figure. Shivam had failed to understand how he, a mere college dropout and an apprentice tailor, could help. With Mahantji's high connections and the increased security ring around the temples and disputed site, he had never considered him vulnerable, not even in this vitiated atmosphere. But they had come for him. Right after those goons scaled the walls and attacked the centuries-old religious structure inside with their pickaxes, hammers, rods and shovels, the masjid defenders had come screaming, their blood boiling. When someone pointed a finger at the local man with vermilion stripes across his forehead, the head priest of the famed Hanuman temple, the surging mob had gone manic and decided to make him and his family pay . . . pay with their life. *While he was away at work, mired in thoughts of his girl . . . whom he had also lost. He had run*

*to them . . . but he had reached too late . . . he'd come to know of
the attack too late . . .*

The tears would not stop now.

A charred piece of black burqa was all that was left of
her. Babloo took his friend to the spot where the Farooqui
family had been burnt alive in their Maruti van. 'Bhaiya, I
never wanted to do this. But . . . but,' he blabbered, 'I, I felt
there would be no closure for you, Bhaiya . . . until you stand
here . . . and see for yourself the blackness.'

How right he was. Shivam picked up the burnt burqa
piece—he knew it was hers from the georgette fabric with its
bead design. She had worn this special one that morning, for
him probably. He rubbed the singed bit of the fabric against
his face . . . feeling her one last time . . . *his girl, gone . . . gone,
just when she was about to show him her face.* He knelt on the
road, his head in his hands and wept . . . the rubble around him
mourning with him. *Rubble . . . that's what his life had become.*
First, Ma and Babuji . . . and now, Aaina. Everyone that
mattered to him reduced to nothing. All that remained for him
to carry in the bus out of Ayodhya was Ma's sewing machine.
And memories—how he wished he could leave them behind
too . . . but they followed . . . as did Babloo, two days later.

16

Shivam gets off the bed to start his day all over again. He hasn't slept a wink. So much has come flooding back because he has walked the banks of his memories . . . holding the kurti, hugging it, speaking to it . . . sharing with it things he has not spoken about in a decade. All that was frozen inside, begins to thaw because the orange in his hand is not just a thing of the past, it spells a tomorrow as well. That it exists and has found its way back to him again means just one thing . . . *all is not lost . . . no . . . not yet.* Its return is a divine intervention. Not that Shivam likes to dwell on such things but God seems to have remembered him. Finally! Sprouting hope, renewing a promise he made to a girl ten years ago.

She was there . . . somewhere . . . somewhere near. Yes. If the kurti was there, so was she. The kurti couldn't have survived without her. She had been wearing it when Babloo left her . . . when Babloo thought he'd seen her in that car that was set ablaze. Its return is surely a divine intervention.

Buoyed by the thought, he walks up, not to the kitchen but to the mirror instead—the cracked and dusty piece of glass that hangs above the sink in the tiny bathroom. He is in no hurry to brush his teeth. He needs to inspect his face, to check if any signs of aging lines have cropped up while he was not looking, not taking care. Suddenly it matters again how he looks. He examines his brows, his nose and lips. They look, more or less, the same, no wrinkles there. Then he goes closer to the mirror, peers in and gets disconcerted—tiny lines have creeped up around his eyes, a gift of the long hours of sewing, squinting to thread the needle, poring over intricate work, straining his eyes, often in dim lighting. *Well, he can't help that . . . she will understand.* But what about that youthful glow and muscular frame that set him apart from the rest of the teens in Ayodhya? That has dissipated. His skin appears tired. *That lost radiance . . . she will bring it back.* He smiles as he tells himself this. He decides to do away with the scruffy beard to regain his clean-shaven look of yesteryears.

His small room in Trilokpuri Basti in Mayur Vihar, where he lives alone, seems to be bursting with hope, optimism and happiness. Even the sunrays seem brighter. Shivam talks to the kurti as he sips his tea. Asks why it took so long for it to arrive . . . *did it not miss his touch . . . his . . .* Suddenly, he remembers something and, putting down the tea glass, he scampers up to the front door and pokes his head out.

'Babloo . . . Babloo!' he screams, calling out to his neighbour. 'Babloo!'

'Coming, Bhaiya,' replies the familiar voice. A minute later, Babloo walks up to Shivam's door. The tailor pulls him inside and locks it.

'What happened, Bhaiya?' asks Babloo, baffled and worried.

Shivam picks up the kurti, holds it proudly in front of him and looks up at his childhood friend, with expectation. His eyes twinkle, leading on the other to remember, to recognize.

Babloo stares, scratching his head, staring at his friend, and then the kurti, thinking . . . could it be . . . no, it could not . . . but it looks . . .

'Yes, it is,' confirms Shivam, grasping where Babloo's thoughts are taking him.

'Aaina?' There, he has said it. Scared, not wanting to, but goaded by his friend, he has mouthed what is on his mind.

Shivam nods. Too overcome to say more.

Babloo blinks in disbelief, not sure what to make of it. The passing decade shows more on him than on his older friend. The one family member he had—his grandmother, died of a heart attack two days after the masjid fell. Babloo migrated to Delhi soon after, to his friend and in hope of a musical career. Over the years, he has seen Shivam disintegrate. He has also seen his own playback singing dreams fizzle into paid performances at local *jagratra* events. His soulful devotional renditions are in demand, but he hates the acts, viewing them as a big let-down to his ambition. Added to all this, he also bears his wife's constant tantrums and the burden of her upkeep—she demands costly face creams and new suits every two months in the false belief that they'll improve her looks. Even her sister stays with them. He had foolishly promised to get her married and is stuck with it. No wonder Babloo has aged more than Shivam, who seems to have lived in pause mode . . . until now.

'Yes, it's her,' exclaims Shivam, finding his voice.

Babloo hugs him. What is happening sounds illogical but true. *If it is true, he won't mind singing in all the jagratras of the world forever.* That smile on his friend's face and the return of his glow . . . it makes him smile and even sing in happiness.

Shivam fills him in on how the kurti landed at his shop as the two of them sit next to the bed, cradling their glasses of freshly made tea.

'What will we do now, Bhaiya?' Babloo asks.

'Find her . . . what else?' Shivam replies.

'And what will you do when you find her, marry her?'

'If I can . . . if she will let me . . . ' His voice falls a few notches as he says this, realizing suddenly how things could have changed with her. Things might not be as smooth as he hopes.

'Arrey, Bhaiya, we'll keep a watch on her, like we did then. Then beg and plead with her to come with us. For always.'

Shivam is laughing now. And Babloo with him. All their doubts drown in that joyful memory from the past.

'Bhaiya,' adds Babloo, sometime later, 'she wasn't available even then. Yet you went after her and got her, didn't you?'

Shivam nods.

'Her Abbu couldn't stop her then. How will anyone now?'

Shivam hits Babloo hard on his back. This singer has become logical and brainy overnight.

'What did your wife feed you last night?' he jokes, aware that Babloo cringes at the mention of her.

'Kya Bhaiya, I was thinking what all we'll do when you get her . . . and you spoilt my mood.' Short-tempered and immature, Babloo's wife is always after him for something or the other.

'I'll . . . I'll take her back to the Sarayu . . . to the river and its banks . . . the lanes and bylanes where she grew up . . . and I . . . and we'll explore them together again.'

'Wah! Bhaiya. I'll come with you too.'

'Your *biwi*? Shivam ribs him again. 'She likes city life . . . she won't go.'

'Good, this will be the perfect excuse to leave her behind then,' says Babloo. Both of them laugh some more, tickled by the idea of him being rid of her.

'Bhaiya,' Babloo gushes on, 'our lives will become opposite na . . . you getting your girl, and I getting rid of mine.'

A loud rap on the door forces them to put a pause to their mirth. Shivam gets up and opens the door.

'Neeta?' Babloo's sister-in-law is at the door, with a steel bowl of something in her hand.

'Babloo, he's—' Shivam starts saying something.

'No,' she stops him mid-sentence. 'It's you I want, you know this.' And she offers him the bowl she's carrying.

Shivam opens the door wide. Babloo waves to her from where he is sitting on the floor.

'Oh . . . oh!' She is taken aback to see her brother-in-law there. Embarrassed, she turns on her heels and leaves, taking her bowl back with her.

This sets off the boys again. Life is suddenly looking up. It is as if things are going back to how they used to be in the past.

'Bhaiya,' Babloo manages to gasp in the midst of all their laughing, 'one more thing you will have to do when you get your girl—'

'—Keep her far from this *churail*,' Shivam interrupts, knowing exactly what his friend is going to say.

Even as they laugh, Babloo makes a serious face. 'Yes, this witch . . . she got her fangs in you big time . . . we got to keep her off Aaina.'

'We'll leave her here in Delhi with your wife Madhu na,' Shivam reminds him.

'*Madhumakhi*!' Babloo corrects his friend.

Shivam begins clearing the tea glasses. It is getting late. He has to leave for the shop. It is an important day.

'Go back to your madhumakhi now,' he orders Babloo, showing him the door. But his friend has some questions.

'Bhaiya, will you follow the driver when he comes to collect the kurti? Or did he mention his address in the measurement slip?'

Shivam shakes his head.

'No, I'll just get her address.'

'What if he won't divulge?'

'We'll do a narco test on him . . . like they do in that *Crime Branch* you watch on TV,' teases Shivam. And he shoos Babloo out before the guy can annoy him further with questions.

17

There is a song in his heart as he lifts the shutters to *Aaina Boutique* this morning. The guard strolling in the apartment compound catches the shift in his mood and looks at him with interest. Munjal is staring too but checks himself from crossing over to find out what is brewing. He has been dismissed by that two-paisa tailor way too many times for his bruised ego to ignore.

However, there is a change on the tailor's side this time.

'Chacha!' Shivam saunters over to his neighbour. 'Guard Bhaiya, looking dapper today,' he says cheerily.

The guard looks carefully at the darzi from head to toe for a sign of some ailment or black magic.

'It's the same face and the same uniform you see me in every day.'

'I'm seeing with new eyes, maybe,' replies the tailor weakly, realizing that the joke is on him.

'Not just new eyes, you got a new face too,' observes Munjal. 'You look really innocent without that beard.'

The compliment makes him blush. Now, this is too much for Munjal to digest. He has to get to the bottom of it.

'Did you get swapped with your identical twin?' asks the older man. He's probably thinking of the kind of photocopy he has in his business.

'I've made peace with my life,' answers Shivam and returns to his shop with a smile, giving the other two enough to chew on.

However, as the hours pass, Shivam's smile fades. It is time to close shop, yet no Honda City has come to pick up the kurti package. *Why? Yesterday, it had been so urgent . . . and today no one has bothered to collect it . . . Is something wrong? Has she . . . forgotten about the kurti? No, she couldn't have . . . must be the driver, the idiot must not have reported for duty today.*

Shivam's mind goes into a spiral, riding first one horse and then another, whizzing past so many thoughts, only to end up in a daze.

He flounders through the night and the next day somehow, waiting. Customers come and go, cars stop and drive away. But the Honda and its driver do not appear. Babloo checks in with him as soon as he gets home.

Shivam goes looking for the car the next day. He asks around for the driver, assuming he works in the neighbourhood and must live close by. He checks from one apartment complex to another, asking, corroborating, and drawing blanks. He goes from pillar to post. When he is about to give up, in a stroke of luck, he ends up at a chemist's shop and finds the man he has been looking for entering it. It seems God has finally switched over to Shivam's side.

Shivam follows him into Anytime Chemist and watches the chauffeur, in plain clothes now, buy a pack of condoms. As he pays for it, stuffs it inside his pocket, and turns to leave, the tailor blocks his way. The driver raises his eyebrows because he doesn't recognize the tailor.

'You came to my shop with that packet of clothes for alteration,' begins Shivam.

'So?' the driver says and tries to brush past the tailor.

'It's done . . . all complete.'

'Fine. Now, tear it,' mutters the fellow and walks out of the chemist shop.

Shivam runs behind him and catches him again on the road.

The driver gets annoyed at this and says, angrily, 'Stop following me, I don't work there any more!'

'But Bhaiya . . . those clothes,' says Shivam softly 'I need my payment.'

At this, the driver stops and laughs harshly. 'I asked for a day off and they couldn't give me that! They'll pay you . . . scoundrels, all!'

'Just give me the address, I'll try,' Shivam prods him.

'B-404, IFS apartments,' barks the driver and takes off.

'B-404, IFS apartments,' repeats Shivam to himself and the night sky.

Then he sprints again to catch hold of the driver, who, by now, is just a far-off blot on the dark road.

'Bhaiya!' Shivam runs up to the man. 'Bhaiya, how does she look, your memsahib?' his voice quivering with anticipation.

'Like rasmalai . . . good enough to eat.' Chuckling, he continues on his way.

Shivam walks back to his scooter, stars in his eyes.

18

Shivam's nights are more alive than his days—his eyes are free to dream of her and his heart bold enough to believe in what the mind conjures up. When he awakes, he is out searching for his dream.

Today, he has reached the IFS Apartments, located strategically near the main road and within walking distance of the colony market, garden and bus stand. This residential complex houses only senior civil service officers and their families. Shivam walks up to the guard's cabin and peeks in to give the flat number.

'Who do you need to visit?' the guard cross-checks.

'I have to deliver the clothes Madam asked me to alter,' he replies, lifting up the plastic bag.

'Wait,' the guard replies as he presses some buttons on the intercom to make a call.

'Hello, a tailor is here for a delivery,' he tells the person on the other end.

Shivam adds his shop location. The guard waves him through.

'Take the lift to the fourth floor.'

Shivam smiles and thanks him. He tries to appear normal. However, as soon as he is past the gate and waiting for the lift, his mouth turns dry and hands get clammy.

Will she recognize him? Will she show it when she does? What if she doesn't . . . It will be Aaina . . . yes, Aaina.

He quells all last-minute doubts and firmly presses the button to call the lift. He can never mistake the kurti. He put his life into it. She wouldn't have given it to anyone, this much he is sure of.

Happy and nervous at the same time, he is overwhelmed and begins to sweat. There's a fan in the lift, he switches it on. When the lift reaches the fourth floor and stops, his palpitations increase. Pulling out a handkerchief, he wipes the perspiration on his face. The years have shaken his confidence. He turns to examine his face again on the steel door of the lift. He sets his hair right. Ready, he looks around for Flat 404 and finds it. There is a Ganesh painting hanging by the door of this flat. There's a name plate too, and on it is engraved: Arvind Gupta.

Shivam's heart is in his mouth. A deep breath later, he presses the doorbell.

The next minute, the door opens and a face peers out.

'How much?' she asks, craning her neck out of the opening. He can see a thin scar running down her left cheek that the curly wisps falling on her face fail to cover.

'Is no one home?' Shivam asks anxiously, craving a glimpse of his girl, if she is there.

'Do I look like a ghost to you?' retorts the girl.

'I only meant . . .'

Before he can explain himself, she opens the door a wee bit more, snakes her hand out, and grabs the bag of clothes from his hand.

'You came to give this na?'

'Is Madam there?' Shivam asks tentatively.

This time, she replies by slipping her free hand inside her blouse to pull out a mini cloth purse. She takes out a hundred rupee note and hands it over to him.

'I want . . . ' Shivam takes it, still trying to engage in a conversation. But the door is slammed on his face.

Shivam is taken aback. This is not how it was supposed to play out. For a minute, he stands there, his mind blank. Then he turns and takes the stairs down and out of the main gate. The guard smiles, watching him leave.

'Madam wasn't there,' he tells the man and stops, hoping to learn more from him.

The security guy only nods. His mouth is full of paan.

'She's not at home or what?' Shivam wants to confirm.

Again, he shakes his head. He dislikes people who expect him to respond when they can see his mouth is busy chewing betel leaf.

So many new doubts spring to his mind now. Shivam dares another question, not realizing he sounds too inquisitive for a tailor and it will only make the guard suspicious. 'Ma'am and sir . . . is theirs an inter-religious marriage?'

Losing his cool, the guard spits out his paan and gives Shivam an earful. 'The people who live here . . . I'm here for their security . . . not to narrate their family lives to passing assholes . . . get it!'

His anger sears through, shutting Shivam up.

'You got your money?' asks the guard, to which Shivam nods.

'Then leave,' the man dismisses him, pointing towards the exit. 'This is the IFS Apartment. Top babus of the Foreign Service stay here. This gate . . . it's there to keep you people off.

Shivam has no rejoinder to this and exits with his head down. He entered with hope and excitement. He leaves with more questions than answers. But it will take a lot more than this to shake him off.

19

Next day, he's back at the IFS apartments, this time in his new purple T-shirt. A different guard is on duty today. Shivam does not approach him. He hangs around a fruit seller, whose cart is parked close to the apartment complex gate, and bides his time making idle talk with the vendor. Cars, as well as people, keep exiting and entering the complex—residents and regular staff breeze through while visitors pause to be screened.

A silver Honda City glides out—the one that dropped off the kurti for alteration. Shivam's antennae go up. He runs to the vehicle and tries to peer in. The windows are rolled up and the glass is tinted. Before the car drives away, the rear window of the car accords him a glimpse of its passengers. Two kids in school uniforms, jumping on their seats. And beside them is this woman in orange . . . a kurti . . . the same one he delivered the day before. Shivam's heart leaps out of his chest. But the car is gone.

What stops by him next is a cycle. It bears the guard who'd shooed him off the previous day. Glaring down at him, the guard barks, 'Are you a terrorist?'

Shivam shifts from one foot to the other, feeling awkward. He stares at the ground.

'This is the second day you are here. What is it?'

'I . . . I just want to meet Madam. I had stitched her kurti.'

'So?'

'So, she knows me,' Shivam says lamely.

The guard gives him such a look of derision that he wilts.

'Yes, she knows you,' repeats the guard, 'she smelt your fingers in those stitches.'

Shivam squirms, the guard's dirty talk making him more uncomfortable.

'That car that just left? She was in it,' Shivam begins to explain. 'Those tinted glasses . . . she couldn't see me. But if she sees me, she will stop to meet me.'

The guard looks at him, top to toe, disdain on his face.

'You get lost, now! Else, I call the cops,' he warns him. Shivam moves away.

The guard takes out a paan from his pocket, puts it in his mouth, and savours it before pedalling on to duty.

* * *

In their two-room tenement in Trilokpuri basti, Babloo's wife, Rashmi, sits, chopping vegetables. Half of this front room is occupied by a bed and a cupboard, while the rest of it functions as a kitchen and living room. A living room because it boasts of a television set and a few cushions on the floor that work as a sofa. The tiny space with a door at the back leads to the other room. It is barely large enough to hold a bed, a few storage trunks and Babloo's music equipment. A medium-sized toilet, with adequate water supply, situated opposite the kitchen, is the one luxury Rashmi enjoys over many of her neighbours.

Rashmi's sister, Rekha, is looking out of the window. The parked bikes, vending carts and the heaps of refuse in the bylane outside don't interest her. It's the lock outside Shivam's door that gets to her. He's gone so early today. And she knows for certain that he is not headed for his shop. She mulls over it. Then when she can't hold it, she blurts out her thoughts to her sister.

'He's gone . . . in that new T-shirt . . . the purple one.'

'Did you see him leave?'

'I heard his bike and checked. But too fast he was.'

'You must be right,' Rashmi responds gravely, 'It is a girl.'

'I told you before. All this shopping–*vopping* . . . it had to be a girl.'

Her sister sounds so glum, Rashmi stops chopping to console her. 'But it's not proven, is it? He's not the Romeo type. Maybe we're jumping the gun,' she suggests, trying to be more positive.

'You ask your husband na,' Rekha whines, 'he'll know for sure.'

Rashmi laughs. 'You think he'll tell me? No way.' She shakes her head. 'Those two are thick as thieves.'

'I'll ask Shivam then,' replies her sister, with some determination.

Rashmi is not taken with this idea either. 'That won't help. He will definitely not tell you,' she says. 'Your Babloo *jija*, okay, there are times he hides things too but he doesn't keep things to himself. Sooner or later, they come out. But Shivam is different. He won't speak a word about what is going on with him. Sometimes I wonder how Babloo, with his silly bhajan singing, is his friend. Both completely opposite.'

'Silly bhajan singing?' screams Babloo from the bathroom. He has been listening to the conversation about his friend and feels hurt that his livelihood is being dragged in. 'Come to my show and see. The public goes mad dancing.'

Rekha giggles and looks at her sister.

'Show!' Rashmi screams back to the bathroom door. 'Don't call your *Mata ki chowki* a show! As for public . . . it's their love for the goddess that makes them sway . . . not your loud, tuneless singing.'

The husband-wife fight does not end there. Rashmi rages on. 'You are a fraud! You made me believe I was marrying a DJ! And what did you turn out to be? *Bhajan mandli ka* bandmaster! Singing paeans to deities in the mohalla. DJ, my foot!'

Babloo waits for her to stop shouting. Only then does he risk stepping out of the toilet. He makes a wry face at his wife, who is back to chopping vegetables with a vengeance. Rekha lolls around on the cushion, enjoying this daily comedy show. The Hindi news blaring on TV isn't half as entertaining.

20

Shivam sits inside an old Ganesh temple that faces the road. The place is so compact that there's space only for God, his priest, and a couple of devotees to squeeze in. Perched near its entrance, Shivam takes care not to block the view of passing devotees, who pause before the enthroned deity, hands folded, offering their prayers and few precious minutes of their busy day.

The mahant's son from Ayodhya is here for reasons not so holy. Blessed by Ganesh, he gets an undisturbed view of everything that goes in and outside the IFS apartments from here. One thing still obstructs his vision though—he can do nothing about the last memories he has of Aaina. She flits before his mind's eye . . . again and again—her blue eyes mesmerizing him, calling out to him, as she goes down that other lane, in the opposite direction, the one taking her home as riots roil the town. She does not want to go, he can see it in her eyes. She's scared and her eyes grow larger and more intense, beseeching him to come along. He can't . . . nor can he stop her. She has to go without him. She's about to disappear . . . no, she can't . . . he won't let her, not this time . . . no . . .

A loud screeching of brakes near him hurtles him back into the present.

It's that Honda City. It's back, braking abruptly at the speed breaker before the apartment complex. In a flash, Shivam is up and sprinting across. He reaches the car, running past the guard room, right as the passenger door opens. Memsahib steps out. Orange, the same orange flashes before his eyes as Madam swings first one foot out, then another, to stand before him, in the kurti he sewed.

'You!' both shout out at once, recognizing each other. It's not the memsahib but the maid—the curly-haired woman who had handed him the money. Neither can figure out why their paths have crossed again.

'How dare you!' Shivam suddenly becomes angry. 'That's Madam's kurti. How dare you put it on!'

Shocked to see that tailor here again, screaming at her, the maid gets angry and cries out, 'Guard!'

The guard is already running up to them.

'You are here again?' he scolds Shivam, 'I'll have to dial the police now.'

'Yes, call them,' Shivam responds angrily. 'This woman,' he points to the maid, 'she's a thief, she is . . . look! This is memsahib's kurti she's wearing, even now. How dare she!'

The guard looks from one to the other, puzzled by the kurti business.

'Ask her . . . ask her, whose kurti it is,' prods Shivam, still not in control of himself.

'Yes, it's Memsahib's,' admits the maid. 'So? So what? She gave it to me.'

Irritated, she now turns to the guard, 'He's a nut case, remove him from here. If memsahib knows of this, she'll . . . '

'Memsahib knows me,' interrupts Shivam. 'Call her, she'll tell you. I . . . I had sewn this kurti for her. I swear, the minute she sees me, she'll tell you who I am. Just once . . . just once call her. 'He is pleading now.

The maid gives him such a look that even the guard concludes that this tailor is crazy and something needs to be done about him.

'You don't bother memsahib, I'll see to him,' he assures her and pulls Shivam towards his room.

Shivam follows the guard outside but refuses to leave. Like a statue, he stands under the sun on the pavement opposite the complex, his gaze stuck on the B wing entrance. Even the guard's heart melts seeing him. He walks up to Shivam again, wanting to knock some sense into his head. 'She's Gupta sir's madam,' he warns. 'He is a very senior officer. Sometimes, London . . . sometimes, America. One snap of his fingers and you'll go flying . . . so don't loiter here. Listen to me, leave before he gets wind of it.'

'Just once, call her. She knows me,' he repeats himself.

The security man gives up. It no longer bothers him that Shivam is standing there. He deserves it.

Another hour goes by. He sees the fellow gaze on, unblinking. Something has to be done. Two drivers in the building are discussing it too. If the building secretary gets to know about him, he will fire the guard. Scared, the guard picks up the intercom and punches some numbers.

'He's still here,' says the guard to the person on the other end. 'You'll have to tell her, I guess.'

Ten minutes later, Shivam sees the maid march out of the B wing, followed by someone. That someone is tall and stately, with hair that even when tied-up goes way down the shoulders, flowing alongside her chiffon dupatta. She has a glowing complexion and is a vision in scarlet is. His heart skips a beat as he strides up to the entrance one more time. As she walks closer, he stares at her, his gaze fixed on her eyes.

'What do you want?' she shouts when her maid points him out. 'What's your problem?'

'Your eyes . . . ' he begins walking up to her for a closer look, 'they aren't blue . . . why?'

She slaps him hard then. And barks at the guard to throw him away.

21

L oud film music overwhelms the senses of those who visit *Shankar da Punjabi Dhaba,* as does the aroma of spicy north Indian food, onions, green chillies and fresh coriander. This roadside eatery, with its metal tables and creaky wooden chairs, is where Babloo meets his friend after he returns depressed from his day-long vigil.

His head swaying to the number that is playing, Babloo considers his friend's forlorn face and thinks about the time that has passed and his friend's die-hard attempts to turn back the clock. The waiter puts two glasses on the table—one with whisky and another, a steel glass topped with lassi.

'Bhaiya,' says Babloo, once the waiter has left their table. 'You got back that kurti like a blast from the past . . . I too am happy about it. But . . . but Bhaiya, that was just a flash from the past. Do you really want to catch up with her again?'

'Abey, what sort of question is this,' retorts Shivam. 'You know what I want.'

'I mean, so many years it's been now, who knows, she might have got married . . . even got kids . . . '

'That kurti, Babloo, you know when it came back to me? Sixth December! Ten years later, but on the same date. You know what that means?'

Babloo whistles, fate has its own twisted sense of humour. 'Bhaiya,' he tries to explain this, still sceptic, 'I want things work out just the way you want, but . . . ten years is a very long time.'

'Till two days back, I was living life like a zombie. I could feel nothing,' says Shivam. 'I would sit alone. I slept alone. And every morning, I would ask myself, are you alive, or just breathing? I felt I was just filling my stomach uselessly.' He pauses, staring out at the road, lost. Then he gathers himself and turns to his friend again. 'But since the time I saw the kurti again, I haven't questioned myself.'

Babloo understands. His friend's love may be the stuff of movies, defying time and the practicalities of life, but it is real. He looks in amazement at Shivam, who has always been his hero, and heroes, well, they do things differently. Shivam's words touch something raw within him; the singer picks up his glass and guzzles down the amber liquid. Shivam turns to his lassi and sips on.

'Okay, decided . . . we go find her. Wherever she is . . . no choice . . . we got to find her,' declares the friend.

Shivam does not react.

Shankar, the pot-bellied dhaba owner is at their table with another bottle of whisky. He tries to pour some into Babloo's glass.

'Arrey stop! You want to empty my pocket, Shankar,' cries Babloo, raising a hand to stop him.

'This one's from me,' the dhaba chief says.

The musician's brows rise to question the free peg.

'You filled Ravi's application form na,' he reminds Babloo. 'Because of you, my brother got that job in Dubai.'

'*Wah*! International bhai you got now.'

'What, Bhaiya,' the dhaba owner waves off Babloo's description. 'He is a desi *halwai* only, there too. Cooking same things as he did in this dhaba. He's got the foreign tag, that's all.'

'Arrey, he must also be getting foreign wages,' teases Babloo, 'he is now a *bada aadmi*.'

'They call him assistant chef.' There is pride in Shankar's voice. 'Pay is good too.'

Babloo slaps the chef on the back to congratulate him and raises the glass to the assistant chef. Grinning, Shankar moves on to attend to another table.

A sombre mood descends on the table once again. Shivam's crestfallen face deflates the high whisky gives his friend. Babloo leans, searching his friend's face for a glimmer of hope, some happiness. But he doesn't find anything. He recalls another face . . . that could bring a smile to his friend's face and, at the thought, himself smiles.

'You sit smiling. My sorry state is funny now?' Shivam is annoyed.

'Arrey, Bhaiya, you'll smile too when I tell you. I've got an idea to get to Aaina.'

Shivam's face perks up. He sits straighter, waiting to find out more.

'No. I won't tell you now,' Babloo goes all secretive. 'I'll take you to him.'

22

It is like the 1990s all over again. That's how Shivam feels when he steps into a cubicle of an office in Paharganj. A large desk and a man seated behind it—he keeps—half-revolving in his high-backed chair—fills almost the entire space inside. *Why the hell is he wearing a hat in here?* This is the first thing Shivam thinks as he slides into one of the two wobbly chairs facing the desk, but he keeps his mouth shut. He needs to be on the right side of this man, who could turn his fate around, or so Babloo promises. And no, he is not an astrologer. Or a tantric skilled in devious arts.

'I am Khanna,' announces the middle-aged, surprisingly fit man, extending a hand to his visitors.

'Me, Babloo. He, Shivam,' beams Babloo, discarding his namaste to accept the handshake.

Target Detective Agency reads the board pinned on the wall behind the man heading the agency.

'Saxenaji must've called you . . . ' says Babloo, after the introduction.

'Yes . . . yes,' says Khanna with a nod. 'Tea or *Coca-Cola*?'

'Nothing, Khannaji. We need to discuss a delicate task.'

'I've handled 186 cases till date,' proclaims Mr Khanna. 'Success rate 100 per cent.'

'That's why we're here.'

Khanna smiles and fixes them with a 'tell me all' look.

'Matter is that Shivam Bhaiya here—'

'— wants a spy on his wife, 24x7?'

Before Shivam can open his mouth, Babloo shakes his head furiously.

'Affair, then? Any background check you are looking for?'

'No . . . no,' says Babloo. 'We want to know about a kurti . . . a girl's kurti.'

'Na . . . na.' It's Khanna shaking his head vigorously this time. 'You want me to put my hands inside womenswear . . . na . . . na . . . that's risky.' His eyes are twinkling though.

'Khannaji, this case is different . . . very different from what you handle.'

The detective sits straighter, adjusts his hat back, and tries to read Shivam's mind while the tailor sits mute beside his friend.

'You see, we got a kurti,' continues Babloo. 'All we want to know is whose it is.'

Khanna looks puzzled. He cannot make head or tail of this case.

'Bhaiya,' Babloo elbows Shivam, 'you tell him the full story.'

Shifting in his rickety seat, Shivam slowly gathers himself, looks at the detective in the eye and spills out his love story, a story that ended just when it began.

Khanna sits listening, his hat masking his reactions as he hears the tale.

'Okay, so the kurti is yours but the woman who's got it now is not your woman, right?' Khanna asks Shivam after the story.

'But she can lead me to my girl . . . '

'Ah! That's where I come in,' Khanna finally gets a grip on his role.

'Those people are big, Khannaji,' Babloo points out. 'Too big. We don't have any access.'

'So you want me to be your ladder.'

The man is sharp. Babloo is now sure he is the man for this job.

'You got to save my friend, Khannaji,' Babloo pleads. 'This guy's been a zombie for years.'

This ego-massage helps. Babloo had learned this in his trade. He has wrangled many performance opportunities from people in authority in this way. Right now, this private investigator, with his expertise and contacts, is the power centre.

'Twenty thousand.'

Two words, but how they make the two visitors jump.

'Tww . . . twenty thousand,' stammers Shivam, and turns to look at Babloo. His friend has brought him to the wrong place.

Babloo stiffens. The quote for the detective's fee has taken the air out of him.

Khannaji of *Target Detective Company* dismisses his not-so-rich clients with a polite 'Come back when you're ready', and turns to attend to his ringing phone.

* * *

'Why were you calling my office so many times?'

Startled, Mrs Gupta spills a blob of nail paint on her toe.

Her husband has walked into the room suddenly and raised his voice, when her whole mind and both hands are preoccupied with painting each toenail evenly.

'Scare me,' she cries. 'Ya! Come, you too scare me.'

Mr Gupta takes off his coat and tie and goes into the washroom to freshen up. He is not in the mood to be drawn into a dramatic argument right after returning from work. It has been a particularly busy day for him, with two foreign delegations in town. Added to the mix were his wife's umpteen phone calls. It was embarrassing to have her calling him again and again even though his secretary had informed her he was busy.

The frazzled diplomat heads for the shower. Years of service in the IFS have earned him silver wisps that fall on his forehead every time he bends his head. A small paunch is the only eyesore on an otherwise broad and muscular frame that he maintains with walks and workouts, whenever he is not travelling for work.

Cool and refreshed after the shower, he reaches for his nightshirt and suddenly recalled something his wife said earlier. *Scared? What had scared her? Was that why she had been calling him continuously?* Concerned, he gets ready in a rush.

'Tell me now, what's riling you?' he asks her, buttoning up even as he speaks.

She sits unresponsive on the bed, watching her nails dry.

'Arrey, Mrs Gupta,' exclaims the diplomat, cuddling up to her on the bed. He draws on his professional expertise to soothe and sweet-talk her till she spills what is bothering her. She tells him about the tailor hanging around the apartment complex and asking about 'madam', following her car and wanting to meet her, and fighting with the maid and the guard for it.

This is too much for the officer husband to digest. He is especially tickled by the part where the fan checks out her eye colour and then complains that it isn't blue. Holding back a chuckle is proving difficult.

'Let me also check,' he says, flirtatiously and mischievously, pushing back the curly hair to gaze into her brown orbs. 'I too got the colour wrong, I think. I need to look carefully.'

She whacks his hand off. He chides her for looking sixteen. 'You look so young, Romeos will come buzzing. It's not their fault.'

'I'm serious,' she says, not in a mood to be mocked.

'I'm serious too,' asserts her husband and picks up his magazine.

But she can clearly see that he is not. His head, buried in the magazine, is shaking with mirth.

Irritated, she gets off the bed, walks up to the switchboard and switches off the fan. She knows her husband can't bear the heat.

'Now you're overacting.'

'I'm feeling cold,' she claims.

'You are not coming down with something na?'

'What do you care!' she retorts.

This is going too far. So Mr Gupta walks up to the couch where his wife has perched herself in a huff and gathers her in a warm hug.

'Why is this bothering you so much, tell me,' he coaxes her, all soft, wanting to dissipate her anger.

'You're, right. I shouldn't be bothered,' she says, looking angrily at him. 'I stay here alone most times with the kids. You are always out on your trips and if anyone . . . anyone from the road . . . comes hounding, it shouldn't be such a big problem. He could've attacked me. But why am I even bothered, you say.'

Mr Gupta gets the message. This is serious. Not to be taken lightly.

'He was bloody stalking me!' cries out his wife.

Mr Gupta thinks about it and realizes that his wife is right. Assaults and kidnappings are so common now. Delhi is getting more and more unsafe by the day.

He holds her tighter.

'I'll look into it right away,' he reassures her. 'Now smile,' he coaxes her.

And she does.

The mood in the room lifts immediately.

* * *

An abrupt change in the tone of his voice and behaviour becomes obvious as the detective puts down the phone receiver and addresses his visitors.

'No point in lingering,' he tells them snootily while dusting off an invisible spot from his shiny waistcoat.

'Any discount?' asks Shivam.

'Would half a girl do for you?' chucks back the detective.

Babloo intervenes, seeing his friend's anger shoot up at this derisive comment. 'Forget the discount . . . tell me if you are up to the task.'

'Mission possible ji,' replies the sleuth, in a more amiable tone. Looking Babloo in the eye, he continues, 'Hundred per cent guarantee comes only with 100 per cent advance.'

'Done,' replies Babloo, not batting an eyelid.

Shivam is scandalized but before he can open his mouth, his friend restrains him with a hand.

'Done deal,' checks the investigator once again, his eyebrow lifted.

'Done.'

'Twenty thousand,' repeats Khannaji.

'But I only have . . . ' Shivam blurts out.

'Will be arranged,' cuts in Babloo.

The private eye looks at Shivam, seeking his confirmation. The tailor nods weakly.

'Okay, you manage the fee,' booms the man. 'Meanwhile, I'll make the calls.'

* * *

Mr Gupta is busy dialling a number. The line is busy. He dials again. But it's still busy.

Fifteen minutes later, he gets a call back.

'How you doing, young man,' says Mr Gupta

'Arrey, sir . . . am fine, sir. What can I do for you?'

'I've got a small assignment for you,' Mr Gupta tells the person at the other end.

'Order, sir.'

'You've got to do this yourself.'

'Yes, sir.'

He gives his instructions in a low voice.

'Darzi . . . ' is all the maid hears as she leaves the room after putting down the tray on the table beside the window.

23

Shivam stands in his boutique, waiting. Not for customers but for his friend, Babloo, who soon arrives in an auto-rickshaw. He is grinning.

'Bhaiya, today will go too good.'

Before Shivam can ask, Babloo elaborates. 'Saw no evil today. Both the witches left before I got up.'

Then, eyes twinkling, Shivam slaps his back. Babloo has seldom referred to his wife or her sister by their respective names. Opening the drawer, he takes out his wallet and counts twelve thousand rupees. 'That's all I've got,' he says, handing over the cash to Babloo.

'No tension. Eight, I'll give.'

'How?' asks Shivam.

'Arrey, this show I'm doing tomorrow. I'll get ten.'

Shivam runs out of words. How do you thank someone who stays by you more than your own shadow? He half-hugs him, embarrassing them both.

* * *

Munjal greets Babloo loudly across the road and invites him over. He likes this singer friend of the tailor. But Shivam restrains Babloo with a hand. They have important issues to discuss.

'When will Khanna start our work?' asks Shivam, more confident now that they have the money.

'After payment.'

'He won't cheat us na?' Shivam is so close to his goal and so financially frail that he doesn't want to be disappointed or left without whatever little he has. 'I have waited for long . . . '

'You'll get what you want,' says Kitty, who has suddenly appeared at the shop. 'I've got this gut feeling. Whatever it is . . . you'll get it.'

Just the thing Shivam needs to hear. Shivam throws an arm around her, pulling her to himself, wanting to feel the warmth of her conviction. She moves in close with him, holding the man who has taken her completely by surprise, filling her with sudden happiness.

Munjal whistles. He has seen such a display of affection mostly on cinema screens and on park benches.

Babloo simply stands around smiling. He knows where this display is coming from. His friend is alive again and dreaming, brimming with hope. They are all dreaming of a bright future.

But two customers enter the shop, requiring Kitty to vacate the space.

'Babloo,' Shivam calls out the minute he has finished serving his customers. He jumps right back to the Khanna topic.

'What if he can't deliver after payment?'

'Don't worry Bhaiya, I'll settle things with him first.'

As Babloo turns to leave, Shivam reconfirms with him, 'I hope you are going straight to him?'

'I'll go in the evening. Got to prepare first . . . I have this show tomorrow.'

'Abey,' hits back Shivam, 'stop calling your *mata ki chowki* a show!'

Babloo pretends not to hear him.

The tailor returns to work but doesn't get much done that day. He tries. But he cannot focus. Aaina fills his head. *Her eyes. How they'll open wide when they see him again. After years. Ten years. Will she cry? Will she smile? Will she cling to him again . . . like she had done in the back alley of Masterji's shop that day . . . the day they came together . . . then fell apart . . .*

He cuts the same cloth twice, ruining the piece completely. By evening, Shivam gives up. He can't work. So he switches off the lights, takes his wallet and tiffin, pulls down the shutter, and leaves.

In his head, he is having a conversation with her as he walks. He forgets to get on his scooter and continues walking.

Blue, I was looking for you, he tells her. And the brown memsahib stared back at me. And what if she had blue eyes, asks his girl. Would you take her to be me? He shakes his head. My girl's a bewitcher. None like her. Ever. She laughs. You're sure she did not tempt you? she asks, teasing. He shakes his head furiously.

Kitty's face looms up in front of him, surprising him. No, shocking him. *Kitty? No. Never. He did not give a damn.*

Still, she keeps coming closer. And closer. And suddenly, all goes still. Shivam lies on the footpath. Bleeding. Unconscious.

* * *

One melody after other swims into Babloo's mind as he sits down to eat. He is confused about which one to try for his show the next day. But before he can take a bite from his roti, Rashmi ladles a big spoonful of ghee on his vegetables.

'Are you trying to kill me?' he exclaims.

'How can I, till you don't get my sister married!' she retorts.

'I married you . . . isn't that enough!'

'You agreed to settle her . . . that was our deal,' she reminds her husband. 'Don't change now.'

'Ya . . . ya . . . only I've changed. You stayed nineteen na.'

Withering under his sarcasm, she switches topic.

'This Shivam Bhaiya . . . what's his scene these days?'

Babloo stays quiet.

'It is about a girl, is it?'

His mobile phone rings just then, saving him, or so he thinks.

It is Shivam's number but some woman's voice. Frown lines appear on his forehead. His wife grumbles that he never eats in peace. 'Always singing . . . or talking . . . or . . . ' she stops as she sees her husband break into a sweat, push back the plate, and rise.

'Moolchand Hospital, casualty ward,' she hears him repeat.

Dinner forgotten, he pauses only to count the notes in his wallet and dole out a hurried explanation to his irritated other half.

On his way to hospital, Babloo dials Shivam's number again. It is busy. He sighs in relief. *Shivam is up and talking. Things couldn't be so bad then.*

He reaches the hospital, strides up to the casualty ward and scans the faces in the room. Shivam is missing. *Did they discharge him*? He calls Shivam again to check. His number is still busy. The lone doctor on duty is occupied with an emergency patient. So are the nurses.

Babloo walks out and tries calling Shivam again. *His friend is not such a talker. Why today then?* He bumps into someone, who, like him, is on the phone.

'Kitty!'

It's her. And that cell phone she is speaking into is his friend's. A hundred doubts arise in his head.

What the hell is she doing with Shivam's phone when she's got her own? And where is Shivam?

'Babloo!' Kitty cries, taking his hand. 'What took you so long? I've been waiting here.'

It takes him a minute to process everything. *Kitty was the one who called him from Shivam's phone. And that she still had his phone meant only one thing. Shivam is not in good shape.*

'Where is he?' barks Babloo, getting impatient.

She takes him to another ward, to a far-off bed, where he lies bandaged and pale, wound up in pipes feeding him IV fluids. Babloo looks away.

'They hit him on the head from behind and ran away.'

Babloo is shocked. *This was not an accident?*

'I came to discuss work but before I reached him . . . they did this.'

He runs out of the ward and hails an auto to Paharganj. As he heads to Khannaji, he punches his number on the phone to tell him he is on the way.

'Khanna is gone,' says the boy selling cigarettes outside the locked office.

'Gone?'

'Yes, gone for good.'

'How you know that?' asks Babloo, patting a fifty-rupee note into the boy's hand.

'He got badly beaten last night. Some big officer's wife he was investigating . . . and they came after him. Very, very powerful people . . . so he fled.'

'And he told you all this?' Babloo finds this hard to believe.
'I did odd jobs for him. I know everything . . . '
Babloo dials the detective again. His phone is switched off.

24

'I can do what Khannaji couldn't.'

What is this claim this Gujju girl is making?

He eyes her with suspicion and growing irritation. After a worried night spent on the visitor chairs lined outside the hospital ward, all he wants is his chai and to get Shivam out of there. Not Kitty and her over-the-top ways.

But she stomps in there again, wearing fresh make-up and butting her nose into what is clearly not her business.

'What's this Aaina business?' Kitty asks Babloo the minute she steps into the hospital. 'Aaina . . . Aaina . . . Aaina,' she cries, flailing her arms up and down theatrically. 'When he fell, when he laid half-conscious in the ambulance, he went on and on, Aaina . . . Aaina, like a chant.'

Babloo keeps quiet.

'Who is this Aaina?' she asks again.

He says nothing again.

She puts both her hands on his shoulders as she turns him around and looks straight into his eyes, demanding an answer. Soon, he tells her everything, spilling all the beans about the girl in the burqa who stole Shivam's heart, her kurti returning in a car ten years later, their search for her, going from

Mrs Gupta's apartment to Khannaji's, to landing in the hospital with a broken head.

The story knocked the wind out of her. He sees her face deflate. She is soon pacing the hospital corridor, thinking about what to do next. And she comes back to Babloo declaring, 'Forget Khannaji.' Slouched in his hospital chair, Babloo stares at her.

'You just give me this Gupta madam's number,' Kitty says. 'I can do what Khannaji couldn't. I'm a girl. She'll talk to me.'

'What will you talk about?'

'If she knows Aaina, I'll get it out of her. Simple!'

Babloo does not feel comfortable involving Kitty. But the Gujju girl is too feisty for him to resist. She marches out of the hospital after securing the number.

His phone rings insistently. Babloo ignores it. He knows his wife is calling him to find out when he'll be home. But even he does not know the answer. So, there is no point in taking her call.

The sun has set. Inside the hospital corridors though, it is tough to tell when noon turns into evening. Babloo has been counting the hours because he was told, 'Next twenty-four hours are crucial.' Twenty have passed. There is no change in Shivam's condition.

When he sees the junior doctor from the ward heading towards the canteen, he follows him. As they queue up to order food, Babloo chats with him.

'Your friend is lucky,' says the doctor. 'A few inches to the left . . . and he wouldn't have made it.'

Babloo nods. That rod had meant to kill. That Shivam was still breathing must surprise the hands that attacked him. That rod had come down hard on his friend, Kitty had told him.

'His vitals are all okay,' the doctor reassures him. 'The MRI is also okay. We have to see how this night goes . . . '

Babloo breathes easier. The doctor has painted a more cheerful picture than he expected.

Someone grabs him by the elbow and whisks him to a corner. 'Kitty!'

She looks grim. *Has she come from Shivam's ward? Was he . . . was he . . .*

'It's all over,' she says, her voice flat.

'What?'

'Yes, I . . . '

He can't hear any more because his head has begun to spin. He turns and runs. Into people, objects, and everything that comes in the way. He goes into the ward, past the guard standing outside.

Shivam! Shivam! Shivam!

He veers to a halt by his bed and finds him still hooked to the IV line. Eyes shut, face masked, a sheet over him. And a machine beeping near him.

Babloo grips the bedrail to steady himself. He moves closer, steeling himself to check on his friend. He puts a hand on his forehead. It's neither hot nor cold. He looks hard at him. But Shivam looks the same. The same as he did last night and this morning. And noon.

Then why did Kitty . . .

The guard comes in to expel him. As Babloo is led out, protesting, he bumps into Kitty again.

'You again!' he screams.

Her presence irritates him now, when everything looks bleak.

A bad omen she is!

Kitty retorts caustically, 'Sorry . . . do you know that word?'

Ignoring her jibe, Babloo lines up to talk to the senior doctor who has come out to address the family of another patient. But he doesn't get a chance. *Hell! These doctors don't even have time to tell you if your patient is dead or alive!*

He is fast losing control and is about to accost the guard outside the ward, when Kitty beats him to it.

'*Bhaiya*, I want to check on patient bed number seven. Shivam. Just a peek,' she bargains. 'Will just smile at him and come back.'

The guard melts and motions her in. But Babloo stops her. *Smile at him?* He catches her by the arm. 'What you told me back there . . . in the canteen . . . that . . . that . . . it's over . . . all over?'

Kitty shakes her arm free and gives him an angry look. 'All that later. Let me meet Shivam first.'

'Wait,' Babloo tries to process this, and fails. 'I don't understand.'

'I don't care,' says Kitty, seething. 'You and your obsession with Aaina can wait. She's dead anyway. Shivam is alive.' And she marches in, leaving Babloo in a daze. Slowly, the clouds clear.

It was Aaina she had referred to in the canteen and not Shivam.

Babloo sighs with relief but winces the next minute. *Aaina is dead? This will kill his friend. Kill him just when he was smiling again.* Babloo bites his nails.

Kitty's mood is sunny now. She clearly doesn't care about Aaina. She drags Babloo to a seat outside the ward. 'He's fine,' she reassures him. 'I tried waking him up . . . and he stirred . . . slightly.'

Babloo sits like a statue, letting her words slide off him.

His friend was waking up, she said. But if he was, it was for Aaina. Only her. Aaina couldn't be gone. Shivam would be gone too then.

'I'll make him so busy that he won't think of her. Ever!'

Babloo lets it pass. He knows that is impossible.

Kitty wanting to offload what is on her mind and starts talking again. 'She . . . Aaina . . . Aaina died giving birth, it seems.'

Babloo is startled.

'Yes. Mrs Gupta told me. She died. And so did the baby. Some infection.'

Babloo's eyes are glazed.

'This happened around four years back, she said.'

Babloo becomes agitated. He needs to see Shivam immediately.

The guard's missing. God *is on his side this time.*

Babloo slides to Shivam's bed. His eyes are still shut. Mask, machine, are all still there. He grips his friend's hand and cries silent tears.

A nurse comes in and asks him to leave. He turns to leave . . . but someone holds him back.

He stops and looks down. His friend's fingers are wrapped round his. His eyes . . . remain closed . . . but he sees a tear sneaking down his right cheek.

* * *

The driver has to brake abruptly. The Honda jerks to a stop, mere inches from the man who has run out to the middle of the road, out of nowhere . . .

'What the . . . !' Thrown off-balance, Mr Gupta holds on to the seat before him to steady himself. His wife slides over to clutch him. Frowning, he looks on.

A banner flashes before their eyes:

Save My Friend.

The rascal blocking their way is holding it across his chest.

As the driver swings out of the car door to push him away, Babloo scampers over to Mrs Gupta. Hands folded, he pleads with her across her husband's rolled down window. 'Ma'am, Ma'am, you . . . only you can save Shivam. You know . . . you know his girl, his life . . . Ma'am . . . '

The driver catches him by his neck even as Mr Gupta is dialling the police. But Mrs Gupta stops him. 'Wait.' She is curious about what power she holds over this Shivam. The man in front of them looks too weak and traumatized to be dangerous. Neither the driver nor Mr Gupta dare disobey her. So they park to the side and give Babloo two minutes to vomit out his trashy story.

The story takes them to the hospital.

'This way, Ma'am,' Babloo leads a curious Mrs Gupta and her increasingly irritated husband into Shivam's ward. Bandaged and masked, Shivam struggles to sit up, his hands folded. Even in his sedated, half-conscious state, he recognizes Mrs Gupta at once. And begs for answers. The scene is too melodramatic for Mr Gupta but he keeps quiet.

Mrs Gupta melts at once. The boy's love story pulls all the right strings in her heart. His burqa-girl search beats all the soaps she watches on TV.

'Aaina,' she sighs. 'I don't know any Aaina . . . But . . . I can tell you from where that kurti came.'

Shivam's face falls and lights up again.

'Aligarh,' she says. 'It came from Aligarh.'

'Aligarh?' Babloo echoes, surprised.

'Yes. From my mother-in-law's trunk. She died last year. I found it there.'

'How can that be,' Shivam cries out. 'It was Aaina's . . .'

'Easy . . . easy . . . ' as Babloo tries to calm his friend, Mrs Gupta continues, 'Ma had a caretaker. Could be hers. Ma wore sarees only, not . . .'

'Did you know her?' asks Shivam interrupting her and pushing away his mask. 'Caretaker, I mean?' His voice gets edgy.

Mrs Gupta shakes her head. 'Not really, but all I know is that she was a young Muslim girl.'

Shivam begins to cry. *What his Aaina must've gone through . . . all these years . . . without him.*

The doctor on duty stands next to Mr Gupta the entire time, listening in. Not stopping these visitors. Not asking them to leave. Mr Gupta speaks now. 'Enough,' he tells his wife, motioning her out.

Babloo manages to get the Aligarh address out of Mrs Gupta before she walks out of the ward and their lives.

'Vaishno Society on Ramghat Road,' he tells Shivam.

There is a tiny bird of hope still fluttering in their chests.

25

S hivam is fortunate that he hasn't lost his memory. However, the headaches have also stayed. He has grown used to the constant throbbing in his skull. It has been there for a week. The doctors were sceptical about his recovery after the head injury and kept checking if he could remember things. He can. Clearly. Aaina. No way could he forget her, ever. And Babloo. His friend is always around and does not give Shivam a chance to forget him. As for the rest, they don't matter.

Finally, they discharge him. And he takes an auto right away.

'I've got to check my shop once at least,' he tells Babloo. Instead, he heads straight to the interstate bus terminus.

'Aligarh. One ticket,' he says, with quiet confidence. A little after four hours, he is standing outside a sprawling housing complex on the Ramghat Road. The sun is scorching overhead, so the place is desolate except for a guard who sits slouched at the gate in a vest and lungi. As soon as Shivam approaches him, he becomes alert.

'Where do you want to go?' The guard's eyebrows rise in sync with his question.

Shivam takes out a pad and pen from his pocket. 'Population survey,' he says. The guard is not convinced. Shivam offers to call his senior in the government department and make the guard speak to him. But the guard is still sceptical. Just then, a few monkeys descend upon them and take off with the guard's tiffin box, which is lying beside him on the ground. As the guard goes chasing after them, Shivam sneaks in.

Once inside, Shivam looks around for someone who can guide him to the flat the diplomat's mother used to occupy. He can't see anyone. Before him loom old, discoloured four-storey structures, with water tanks and TV antennae on the roofs. They seem silent and empty of life from afar. Up close, he finds balconies bursting with flowerpots and kurtis, sarees, shirts and underwear hung out to dry. *Wait, he can spot someone . . . A woman, two balconies above him.*

'Hello Madam!' he tries to catch her attention.

Plop! Something lands on his head. It is a garment that the woman is trying to spread to dry. Before it can slip and get dirty, he catches it. He suddenly feels embarrassed because it's a piece of lingerie. He looks up. The woman has gone back inside. Like a fool, he stands there with the mauve strappy bit in his hand.

'It's my Ammi's.' A boy runs up to him and announces.

Relieved, Shivam pulls a sheet out of his note pad, wraps the fallen bra in it and hands it over to the boy, who takes off with it.

'Hold on!' Shivam runs after the kid and catches up with him as he is about to scoot up the stairs.

'Do you know where C wing, flat number 103 is?'

The kid in a Mickey Mouse T-shirt and matching shorts stares pointedly at the pen in Shivam's hand. 'Is that a gel pen?'

'Do you like it? . . . Here, take.' Shivam hands it over to him. 'But help me with the directions, please?'

The boy nods and motions for Shivam to follow him as he races ahead. Shivam tries to keep pace. Two buildings away, on the ground floor, they pause outside a flat. Most of the letters and digits have fallen off from the nameplate and only one digit and letter remain. A heavy metal padlock hangs outside the door. 'This is the one you were looking for,' says the boy. Shivam nods and he rushes off. *So this was where Aaina lived and worked!*

Shivam leans against the locked door, wishing to go back in time so that he can just ring the bell and meet her. In front of him there is another flat and its nameplate says: # 102, VERMA's. Shivam rings the bell. 'Phenyl, acid, soap . . . whatever you are selling, I don't want it!' comes a sharp response. Shivam presses the doorbell again.

A chubby lady in a maroon kurta flings open the door and looks at him curiously. 'What you want?' she asks matter-of-factly.

'Population survey,' repeats Shivam and pulls out his pad.

'No gents are at home right now, come later,' she says as she tries to close the door.

'That's okay . . .' begins Shivam.

'That's not okay!' she says and bangs the door shut.

Shivam is left staring at the locked door. He takes the stairs up to the first floor and climbs down hurriedly the next minute as ferocious barking follows him down. Exasperated, he wanders around the compound till he comes upon a Sardarji washing an old Maruti.

'Me, Surinder Ahuja . . . hello ji,' Sardarji introduces himself with a smile.

Shivam smiles tentatively, trying to frame a question.

'This file . . . pad . . . are you a *sarkari afsar,* a government official?'

Stumped by the Sardarji's acute observation, Shivam nods eagerly. 'I'm here for the population survey,' he reveals.

'Counting people . . . bloody that's an impossible job in India, *hain na*?' he asks laughing.

'Sardarji, I needed info . . . ' begins Shivam, only to be cut by Sardarji, who now leaves the wipers of his car to come close and whisper.

'This colony . . . I tell you, every family is busy making an army! Every flat you see . . . four or more kids . . . every flat.'

Shivam has no answer. He turns around restlessly looking for another person who will talk less and answer more.

The Sardarji stops him as he sees his attention waver. 'Water . . . Has anyone offered you water?' he asks eagerly.

'Not water. I need data,' Shivam tells him.

'Accha, come. Let's go to my flat,' Sardarji invites him. 'My car cleaning is over. You can start your survey with me.'

Shivam follows him.

He notes that the man lives in wing A of the apartment complex. When they reach his house, he pulls out his key to unlock the door and Shivam does a double take. *What the hell is this! A flat or a garage?*

For he can see piston rods, flashy wheel-caps and spanners adorn the walls. In one corner, stands a jack. In the centre of the hall lies a huge tyre, topped with glass. A painting of Guru Nanak Dev, lit up with colourful bulbs that blink constantly.

Shivam looks on, dazed.

His host guides him to one of the Rexine sofas. He picks the deodorant kept by the window and sprays it all over the room 'to freshen it up'. Next, he fetches a pitcher of rose sherbet and pours out two glasses—one for Shivam and another for himself.

'Do you like chicken?' he asks, as Shivam sits sipping the drink.

'No sir, I'm a vegetarian.'

'Oh! I'm a chicken lover.'

Shivam smiles.

'Just three or four Hindu families we've got in the C wing . . . rest are all Muslims.'

'And how many are there in your family, Ahujaji?' asks Shivam, slipping into his role of a population officer.

'One-man army, sirji,' declares the Sardarji. Winking, he adds, 'All this exploding population . . . yaar . . . someone has to show control na.' He looks lost. 'It's not easy to manage alone . . . just that in time, you get used to it.' They sit quietly for a minute, before he perks up again and asks Shivam, 'You tell me . . . you look married, family-wallah types . . . '

Shivam nods.

This sets off the Sardarji again. 'I too got engaged . . . almost.' He pauses to take a sip. 'But then an NRI match came for her . . . Canada wallah . . . and she dumped me. Aligarh can never compete with Canada, right?' He gulps downs the sherbet and his grief. 'Forget all this,' he declares, in his normal tone, 'In your list, put one . . . one member for this flat.'

'And for C wing, 103?' Shivam asks, tentatively. 'It was locked, but I need the information for every flat.'

'103? That's Guptaji's flat . . . Arvind Gupta . . . he's an IFS who stays in Delhi. His mother used to stay here. Auntyji couldn't stand Delhi . . . all that noise . . . the *showbazi* . . . all the hypocrisy of a big town.'

'She lived alone?' Shivam asks casually but his heart thumps with expectation.

'No, no. She had a caretaker . . . a young Muslim girl.'

Shivam is almost delirious with excitement now. 'How . . . how old was she . . . what did she look like?'

'Auntyji?' Sardarji is incredulous at this question.

'N . . . No,' Shivam gives out an embarrassed laugh. 'This caretaker girl that you talked about? It will help in my survey.'

'She wore a hijab. I never saw her face.'

'Her eyes . . . her eyes? Would've been open. Were they blue?'

Ahujaji's fist comes down on the Rexine sofa. 'Arrey I wouldn't know if my girlfriend's eyes were black or brown . . . and you want me tell you if I have peeped into the eyes of a girl who was wearing a hijab and working for an old lady? What kind of a survey is that, *haan*?' He gets up.

Shivam stands up, shaking and disappointed. But he doesn't explain himself.

'Okay, sir*ji*. Got to go now . . . work,' says his host.

As Shivam leaves the flat and makes his way down the stairs, his mind is in on overdrive.

Aaina did stay here. That is almost confirmed. But where was she now . . . where in Aligarh? Did someone here know? Will they tell?

He lingers near the C wing again, his heart unwilling to leave without an answer. He's not sure if he will be able to come back here. He sees three girls, of varying age and height, come down the steps of the Wing. His hopes rise.

'I'm looking for Aaina,' he tells them. 'C-103.'

'C 103 wallahs all are dead,' says one girl curtly. 'It is a gh . . . h . . . h . . . host house now,' she says trying to scare Shivam. The others laugh wickedly.

'No!' Shivam almost screams in irritation. 'Not the old woman, I'm looking for the young girl with her'.

'Young girl?' repeats another girl. 'Ask *Bhaijaan* then . . . he knows every young girl here,' she says pointing to the two boys who were coming towards them. Then, without a warning, she calls out, 'Bhaijaan, he's asking for a young girl.'

Shivam instantly regrets having spoken to the girls. Before he can open his mouth to explain, a hand lands on his collar. The boys stand in front of him, poised for a confrontation.

'Don't do this,' Shivam tries to jerk himself free. He shields his head with his arms. He can't risk another head injury.

The boys don't listen to him. They grab him and tackle him to the ground. 'Young girl, you want . . . young girl na,' cries the taller of the two boys. 'Young boy, I give you. Take!' He kicks him. Shivam turns quickly and rolls off to avoid the blow.

'Arrey, stop. He is a government officer!' says the guard, rushing in. Deaf to the watchman, the boys jump on Shivam, not letting him get up. Bunching up his lungi, the gateman readies to enter the battle. By then, Shivam has regained control and is up on his feet. Those years of body-building and swinging the club in the park . . . these skinny boys are no match for him.

'You guys have got it all wrong,' he says, as he wards off the taller one while holding the other boy with an arm and half his body. 'Aaina, I was looking for . . . only Aaina,' he shouts into their ears.

The words are wasted on them because the lanky boy is in no mood to give up. The watchman sees him land a kick from the back, forcing Shivam to swerve and push him off. The boy stumbles but Shivam catches him before he hits the ground, not wanting the youngster to get hurt.

Drawn by the ruckus, more people descend on them. They start attacking the outsider to save their colony boys. The watchman dances about in his lungi, trying to clear the air. Everyone is spoiling for a fight and no one listens to his pleas.

Shivam is on his knees and six-seven of them rain blows on him. Arms crossed over his head, he sways back and forth, shielding himself unsuccessfully.

'Stop!' screams the guard finally, running into the middle as things threaten to get out of hand. 'He did nothing. Hafiz and Imran started it . . . yes, Hafiz and Imran!'

By the time the throng lets go of him, Shivam is limping. His left arm and lip are bleeding into his shirt. Not sparing another glance at the C wing or its occupants, he hobbles out of the compound, helped by the guard.

'Aaina?' The watchman can't help but ask as he leads the population survey officer to the gate.

'I came for her.'

'Not to count people?'

'No, she's my life,' he tells the guard, hoping the man will understand and forgive him the lie. 'I came here looking for her.'

The guard doesn't say a word. He flags an auto for him and walks back to his perch.

'Navrang Guest House,' Shivam tells the auto wallah, grateful for this help. 'Take it quickly please. I've got to catch my bus.'

His belongings are at the guest house. Only after checking-out from there can he take the bus out of Aligarh.

26

As the auto starts, someone slips in beside Shivam. 'Sardarji!' 'Just accompanying the injured party,' he replies with a smile.

'I'll manage,' protests Shivam.

Sardarji does not budge.

The auto wallah gets confused . . . to go or not to go?

'Please, I want to be alone . . . please, Sardarji . . . there's no need of anyone.'

'Aaina?' His eyes twinkling, Sardarji utters the one word that holds a world of promise. That one word shuts him up.

As the auto turns towards the guest house, Shivam looks at Sardarji but holds back himself from asking what brought the man to him until they reach the guest house. Once they are in his room, Shivam, who has momentarily forgotten that he has to leave urgently, brings it up again. 'You knew her?' he asks cautiously and in anticipation.

'Not as much as you,' replies Sardarji, with a smile. 'Yaar, you should've told me before it's a matter of love-*shuv* . . . all this fight scene would have been cut.'

'Sardarji . . . ' Shivam is impatient but Sardarji has his own leisurely style of speaking and refuses to be rushed.

'I told you na, only three-four Hindu families here . . . in this compound . . . and Auntyji lived alone. So, she called me . . . sometimes to service the AC, sometimes the car. Sometimes, just to talk.'

Shivam nods, realizing he will have to let Sardarji tell the story in his own way.

'And Aaina, your Aaina, would be there all the time . . . fetching something . . . feeding her . . . filling some form for her . . . or dialling the numbers she wanted. Auntyji was a strict lady, kept the girl on her toes.'

'And after her?'

'After her, she went with Abdul. Abdul, our supplier. Everything here, he supplies . . . milk to bread to eggs, even meat. Any electrical problem, we call Abdul. For flat sale also, he . . . '

'Went with him means?' cuts in Shivam, now sick with anticipation.

'Married him, I guess . . . she had nowhere to go after Auntyji.'

'Why Abdul?' Shivam refuses to believe it.

'He came to our colony every day, so she knew him in a way,' says Sardarji. 'She did not know anyone else here, I think. No family also. Where is a girl to go!'

But Aaina was not the sort to tag along with just about anyone . . .

'Are you sure, Sardarji?'

'Wait, I'll get you Abdul's address. You can go and check yourself.'

Fifteen minutes later, Sardarji is gone, having left a piece of paper in Shivam's hand.

Muazzamil Manzil, 23-A, Kabir colony
Shivam takes another auto-rickshaw.

* * *

It is dark by the time he reaches Kabir colony. Once again, he stands in front of a gate. However, this time it is different. The gate is broken and leads up an uneven path to a ramshackle structure that has a door and a few windows—all shut and heavily curtained, the only light is around the edges of the curtains.

He stands there staring at the scene. For an hour. Two hours. Staring, but not a soul leaves or goes into the building. And then, the lights go out too—the lit edges of the curtains become dark. He leaves then, feeling his way back through unknown, unlit lanes, in what is a dark, moonless night. It is too dark, and he thinks he could be misunderstood.

He is back again the next day. This time, he finds the main door of the house partly open. Again, no one exits or enters. He ventures closer and peeks in.

Someone is flitting about in a mauve salwar kameez. He sees her . . . carrying something . . . keeping it and returning . . . leaving again for something else. He tries to get a glimpse of her face but can't see. It's just the whisk of her dupatta flying about her as she moves to and fro briskly. Shivam grows eager. *What if she is indeed his Aaina?*

It looks like no one else is inside. Gathering his courage, Shivam walks up to the unlatched door and calls out to her in a loud whisper, 'Aaina?'

Startled, she drops what she is carrying. Before he can say another word, she slams the door on his face and locks herself in.

'Aaina!' He pleads at the closed door.

'Not here,' she replies from within. 'She doesn't stay here.'

Shivam cannot let go. He bangs on the door, begging her to open it and talk. She does not respond. He then rings the doorbell. There is no answer. He rings it again and again. He knows she's there, standing by the door, on the other side . . . he can hear her.

'Aaina! It's me . . . Shivam,' he says. 'Just open the door and see my face. You'll know.'

Still, she doesn't say a word. The door doesn't open even an inch. He cannot stand at the door indefinitely. So he turns to go. He makes it past the iron gate to the footpath opposite. But his feet refuse to step further. He drops down at the spot, beneath a tree, and sits waiting. Just like he waited for her years ago. She will be watching him. He knows that. And yes, soon he spies a figure peeking from behind one of the curtained windows. He waves to her. Lets her know he's there for her. Waiting till she is ready.

That flusters her. She picks up the phone and dials a number. This is the one thing she wanted to avoid but can't now.

'Someone's at my door,' she says.

'Who's he? What does he want?'

'Aaina,' she whispers.

'I'm coming,' he barks and disconnects.

She shivers as she hangs up. She did not want to make the call but this boy . . .

Under the tree, Shivam sits lost in his thoughts. *He should've seen her eyes . . . somehow, should've managed this. He made it to her door, yet he didn't . . .*

He shakes his head. He tries shaking it again, but can't. Someone has grabbed it from behind.

Shivam sits up straighter and tries to yank his head back from the unseen person's grip. But he is pulled back. Shivam swings around and punches the face he is yet to see. Caught off-guard, the person topples and falls on the pavement.

Shivam looks at the man his Aaina has chosen. A sullen visage, marred by a scar. He is half-lying on the footpath beside him. Shivam is disgusted by his behaviour. *How could she?* He looks so harsh. And older, in his forties, perhaps. Dark and thin-lipped.

As he gets to his feet, Shivam gets up too. 'Get lost . . . you!' This does not scare Shivam. The lean supplier has not half the muscle as him.

'I want to meet Aaina,' he says, trying to placate him.

The man goes berserk. 'Meet her in hell!' he screams and charges at Shivam, pulling a knife out of his jeans pocket. Shivam falters, not having expected this, but escapes the knife. As the two slug it out on the street, a crowd gathers around them. Suddenly, the door of the house opens and a woman rushes out.

'Let him go,' she pleads with the man, trying to break the fight. 'We don't want another police case.'

Shivam lets go of his attacker and turns to look at her. He sees a flash of mauve because, in the next instant, she is dragged away from the scene by the man. But not before he has seen her eyes.

They are blue! The same blue eyes he worshipped.

'Aaina!' He cries out and runs after them.

This time he gets a gash across his arm. Pushing Aaina inside the door, the man attacks Shivam viciously. Someone from the crowd rushes in to save him. When he sees five-six more people walk towards him, the man pockets his knife.

Filthy language follows as Shivam trundles out, his arm bleeding, past the iron gate.

'You need to bandage it,' says the stranger who jumped in to save him. 'Come, I live next door.'

As the neighbour's mother dips her scarf in a bowl of ice water and cleans his wound, she scolds him. 'Why did you pick a fight with him? Don't you know what a butcher he is!'

Shivam keeps quiet. He's hurting. Not from the knife gash but because he can't imagine how she was with this man. *She was so aloof with him but how she came running for Abdul! It kills him to see them together. Why . . . why is she doing this to him?*

'Are you related to Aaina?' The old woman's question rescues him from his depressing thoughts.

He nods.

'Then where were you when she was in trouble and had to run away.'

'Run away?' Shivam is stunned to hear this.

Done cleaning his wound, she nods and gets up. 'Yes, to Dubai . . . didn't you know?'

Shivam looks blank.

'No choice she had . . . This butcher tortured her every night . . . and his wife took revenge during the day.'

This knife cut into him again . . . this time through the heart . . . He is bleeding badly and none can see the wound that will never ever heal . . . never!

Shivam shut his eyes . . . The pain is getting unbearable.

'Are you okay?' The man who saved him from Abdul comes forward, wondering what has suddenly come over Shivam.

Opening his eyes, Shivam begins to put two and two together . . . The first thing that hits him is a realization that is soothing. 'So, this woman here is not Aaina?'

'Aaina? No, she's Rukhsana . . . Abdul's wife,' replies the mother before her son can open his mouth.

'But her eyes—'

'Why you asking all this?' cuts in the neighbour. Shivam's questions are making him apprehensive.

'Am looking for Aaina . . . went to Auntyji's place where she worked. They sent me here.'

'*Beta*, she's gone. Forget her,' says the mother. The old woman can see the grief in his eyes and his shaky voice. She understands where this is coming from.

'But why Dubai?'

'For work. But also because Abdul can't catch her there.' This time, the son answers.

That makes sense. Shivam nods. 'And you would have her Dubai address?'

That is too much to hope for but he gives it a shot.

'Afim bhai, who got her passport, etc., done said she'd got some job there.'

'Afim bhai . . . can I meet him?' asks Shivam, pushing his luck.

'Yes, you can. For this, you'll have to die first and pray you land in the same place as him.'

The neighbour, tired of Shivam and his questions, shows him the door.

With the Afim bhai lead too reaching a dead-end, Shivam does not know which route to take now. The auto wallah deposits him to the guest house. He enters it with a heavy heart. A sad number from the yesteryears is playing on the radio and the receptionist sits humming, his eyes closed.

'Key.'

His eyes snapping open, the receptionist regards Shivam curiously.

'Did you come here to wrestle?' he asks, eyeing the bandages around his head and arm. This is the second time he's seen him beaten up in the past two days.

'Key,' repeats Shivam, not interested in small talk.

'Your brother took it.'

'My brother?' Shivam looks clueless as the receptionist puts up his hands in surrender.

Shivam is sure it is Sardarji, who has come to check how the story went with Abdul. But he is in no mood to talk with anyone. He will simply pick up his bag and leave. When he reaches his room, he finds the door shut. He knocks but no one answers. He knocks harder. Still, no response. That makes him angry. He is tired and in a foul mood. This is the second time in the day that he has stood knocking and people have refused to open the door for him and, damn it, this one is to his own room. He starts kicking at it, raising a racket.

It opens suddenly and he almost falls in as he is leaning against it. Someone supports him as he stumbles and the touch feels oddly familiar. He raises his head.

'Babloo!'

Babloo bends over to pick up his headphones, which have fallen to the floor.

'What Bhaiya! Two songs I was mixing in my head . . . and you ★★★★ed it all!'

Shivam does not react. This is too much. Babloo has always known Shivam to rant, rage or rile at him. Never has he gone silent on him. He looks at his friend closely.

He looks defeated. There are new bandages on his arm.

'Bhaiya, why are you looking like this? One day I'm not there and you go to pieces.'

This familiar banter snaps something inside Shivam. He chucks the bag he is packing on the bed and sits morosely, with his head in his hands.

Babloo sees tears welling in his eyes.

'I'm starving,' he says to distract his friend. 'Bhaiya, let's go eat something first.'

'You are always starving,' Shivam says and smiles. He knows that his friend and his growling tummy can be ignored only at his peril.

It is almost evening by the time they board the UP Roadways bus to Delhi. By then, not only are their stomachs satiated, Babloo's mad talk and reassuring ways have calmed Shivam's mind too.

'You didn't see her? No problem,' says Babloo. 'A new place you saw na. Now you can tell people you've been to Aligarh too.'

Shivam keeps looking out of the window, not adding to the insane chatter.

'And Bhaiya, if this continues, this search, I mean, and you keep getting clues . . . not her . . . just clues to her . . . think Bhaiya, full world you'll get to see!'

One punch from Shivam and Babloo gets even more excited.

'At least Dubai-returned you'll become now . . . 100 per cent . . . that I guarantee.'

'And I guarantee,' Shivam says, 'if you were a girl and I married you . . . I wouldn't have to go anywhere. Except for the bathroom.'

'Bhaiya, you don't like me tagging along right . . . I won't once you get her . . . pucca,' his voice is low now.

Shivam first hugs and then hits him. '*Dramebaaz*! I'm used to you now . . . if you go . . . I'll have to go searching for you also.'

This warms Babloo's heart like nothing else can. This is the first compliment he has gotten out of Shivam in all these years.

'Babloo, this kurti is making me dance so much . . . I wish it hadn't come to me only.'

'You say this one more time and I'll get you hitched to my wife's sister . . . pucca I'll do that!' Babloo threatens him.

The idea is abhorrent . . . and both roll their eyes in disgust.

'Let's book her for next life,' laughs Shivam.

'Yes,' agrees Babloo, adding 'For someone we don't like.'

He is so tickled by this thought that the passenger behind has to poke his head and yell at him to stop shaking so. Shivam goes back to gazing out of his window, staring blankly as another place linked to her fades into nothing.

27

The bus jerks to a stop in the middle of the road and jolts everyone awake.

'Dacoits!' screams someone.

Ten minutes and much chatter later, a plump man boards the bus. In denims and a T-shirt that announces him *World's Best Lover,* he's coming towards them looking like anyone but a dacoit. Three seats ahead of them, he kneels before a girl and confesses his love to much whistling and clapping all around.

As the bus revs back to life and races ahead with the additional passenger, Shivam grips Babloo's shoulder. 'Yaar, I was the one who came seeking a girl . . . and this muffin got one!'

'Bhaiya, we're in UP now . . . You just say . . . in minutes, I'll get his encounter done.'

'Abey, fool! I don't want his girl. My girl, I want only mine.'

'That's the problem. Else I would have lined up six for you. Mine too is on offer . . . only no one takes.'

Shivam turns away. He's not in the mood to banter. He is trying to figure all the roadblocks to Dubai. He needs to clear them one by one. Fast. And leave.

Babloo quits goofing around and sets his sights on the Arab nation too. *Hundreds of things will need to be in place. Passport, visa, cash, contacts* . . . He starts scrolling his phone contacts, one by one. And hits jackpot!

'Got it, Bhaiya . . . Dubai-wallah contact!' His excitement bubbles over. 'Our Shankar na . . . his brother is there . . . now, no issue. Everything he will tell us.'

'Shankar, who?' Shivam asks, curious.

'Arrey, our dhabe-wallah Shankar, the one who was giving us free booze the other night.'

'Okay. The one whose forms you filled.'

'Those were his brother's. He's the chap living in Dubai.'

'Ask him how he sent his brother there.'

'That's the idea. Bhaiya. Let's dine at his dhaba tonight.'

Shivam is smiling now. But in the next second, he gets tense again.

'Babloo, this Khannaji . . . you think he will refund our payment?'

'Now, where will we go looking for him? . . . One more detective you'll need to track this one.'

'Lot of money it was . . . '

'Forget it, Bhaiya . . . it's gone. We will get a personal loan.'

'Personal loan! Which bank will grant us a loan, you idiot!

'Arrey, you don't worry . . . I'll do something.'

'Will you sing for them? Ten paisa you'll get then . . . not loan.'

'Bhaiya, if you want to go to Dubai, stitch your mouth and sit quietly.'

And that's exactly what Shivam does. Not because of Babloo but because he needs to be with himself and sort things out. The past three-four days have seen more action than the whole damn decade. And more is yet to come.

Before the bus reaches Delhi, a phone call changes all plans for dinner at the dhaba.

Mr Chaddha wants to take Babloo with him to London, and he wants to meet him immediately about this. The NRI client will pay big money and wants to meet and discuss the details.

'My ears are rotting with this *virgin* . . . *like a virgin* all the time. Any party in London I go to, it's the same . . . Madonna–Prince, Madonna–Prince. Indians there all turning angrez, *saale!*'

Babloo does not interrupt to ask Mr Chaddha why he lives in England if he hates the English so much.

'Not on my birthday. No pop-*shopp!* I've told my wife that I want only desi stuff in my party. Dhawan saheb recommended you then. *Dhamaka*, he called your bhajans . . . total filmy touch wallah singing! Exactly my taste! So, I'm booking you for next month . . . quote your fee. I'll give fifty per cent advance now. Plus for tickets . . . visa, etc.'

Is this a prank? Only Shivam Bhaiya tries such stunts on him. It can't be Shivam. He's sitting right next to him. He's gazing out of the bus window while Mr Chaddha calls for an appointment. Insisting for tonight only. At Taj Hotel. It isn't a prank!

Babloo rubs his eyes to make sure Mr Chaddha is real.

Three quarters of the next day disappears in listing the Bollywood numbers Chaddhaji especially likes. Babloo will prepare his remixed bhajans accordingly. He is made to sign a proper contract for the show.

'No advance can come without a contract . . . business is business,' booms the NRI as his secretary readies the necessary papers.

Cheque in pocket, Babloo came down the hotel lift, whistling. He feels rich. Shivam does not believe what Babloo narrates till he flashes the cheque.

'Life is insane yaar,' Shivam remarks, as they leave the hotel. 'First, muffin gets girl . . . now, you get paid for shrieking.'

'Bhaiya, I'm telling you . . . , once, I'm gone, you'll miss my voice.'

'You are right. I'll keep your . . . recording, I'll keep . . . to scare my kids. Now, quiet.'

They go to the bank to deposit the cheque in complete silence. In their excitement, they forget that it was way past banking hours. Both are busy thinking. Planning. *I will sell my shop . . . everything here . . . except . . . except the sewing machine. Not Ammi's machine. Everything else . . . This should take care of the ticket and travel . . .*

Babloo is smiling as he rides pillion. Seventy-five thousand rupees is big money. And this is only half the advance. Best part is that his wife knows nothing of it. He could blow it all up as he chooses! And he will, right away!

Shivam brakes suddenly.

'Yes, kill us,' screams Babloo, 'kill us just when things start looking up.'

'Kishore Kumar, control! This high volume . . . and you won't make it to London. Your throat will go on strike.'

Babloo calms down. Shivam knows his buttons and also knows when to press them. The bank is closed, so they travel in a daze onward to the dhaba. Both of them are not hungry, even though neither has eaten anything since a while. It seems a happy turn in life fills not just their minds but their stomachs too. Once at the table though, they devour all the freshly cut onion rings the waiter places before them in a metal plate, dipping them greedily in the bowl of green mint chutney served alongside.

'You are both famished!' laughs Shankar, noting that they had not waited for the meal to be served before polishing off the onions.

'Yes, for you.' And catching the dhaba owner by his billowing shirt sleeve, Babloo pulls him over to the empty chair at their table.

'Arrey, it's business time,' protests Shankar. 'I can't sit.'

'Sit for two minutes. I need a favour today,' Babloo says softly. 'A big one.'

'No stress, bhai . . . pay next time.'

'It's not that . . . this favour is bigger.'

Shankar eyes him warily. 'See, I can't give a loan. Sending Bunty to a foreign country you know ate up whatever little I'd saved.'

'Relax, Shankar bhai. No one's asking for a loan.'

The man breathes easier.

'Like you sent Ravi, send my brother too,' he say pointing to Shivam. 'He also wants to go. Same place.'

'Dubai?'

Shivam nods.

'I told him Shankar bhai's the expert on Dubai.'

Pumped by this praise, the dhaba owner readily spends over fifteen minutes with the two, guiding them on how to get the passport done quickly under the Tatkal scheme, which Karol Bagh agent to go to for the cheapest ticket, and details on other documents required for travel.

'Once there . . . eat, work, enjoy . . . do all . . . but keep one thing in mind, keep far away from girls. The Arabs have got very tough laws. So, no staring, no talking . . . have absolutely nothing to do with them.'

'Arrey he's going after a girl only.'

'What!'

Shankar is shocked but he cools down when told about the love angle. Then he continues, 'Food you'll have to manage . . . lodging your employer will arrange.'

'What job? He's chucking all he's got here to go searching for his girl.'

Some guest creates a racket over his half-baked roti and the dhaba owner is summoned to pacify the customer. He returns to Babloo's table right after he sorts out the issue, curious to hear more of this love angle. And when they tell him the whole story, he becomes emotional.

'Yaar, I'll ask Ravi if you can stay with him for a few days,' he offers.

Overwhelmed by his generosity, Babloo hugs him. 'You speak to your Ravi . . . and I'll get his documents done.'

* * *

'I love you, Chaddhaji . . . ' Babloo sings in his sleep.

'Chaddhaji?'

His wife, who has no ear for his songs, jolts awake.

Babloo curses himself. Chaddhaji has to stay a secret from wifey. He can't tell her that the first international assignment he has is being harvested to fund his friend's passport, ticket and visa. She would explode.

'Songs . . . I like his songs . . . he's the new singer on the block . . . Chaddhaji.'

She falls for that line. Her husband goes gaga over one singer or the other all the time. An impending marital war is thus nipped in the bud. Babloo snores until sunrise, content with all he has managed the past week.

Dawn brings another problem with it. The problem of more funds and this time the solution is complicated. Babloo lies in bed chewing on it. This is not an easy decision for him. But by noon, Shivam and he reach the goldsmith.

'This is a pure gold set, a good design too,' he says after his discussion with the jeweller. The jeweller picks up one bangle and eyes it closely, not taking Babloo at his word. He scratches its surface on a stone, pours a drop of something on the yellow metal and then blows on it. His face gives no clue about his finding. Then, he takes it the set inside to his assistants for an evaluation. Babloo and Shivam wait patiently until one of them returns with the details and whispers in his master's ears.

'Seventy seven thousand for the set,' he announces after his assistant leaves.

'It's worth at least eighty-five, I can guarantee you that.'

'Life has no guarantee, you are talking of this . . . '

Shivam does not like this smooth-talking jeweller at all.

'Eighty-three?' Babloo bargains.

The jeweller keeps the set gently on the table.

Shivam nudges Babloo. 'He's looting you. Let's go . . . we'll do something else.'

'Give your last price,' tries Babloo, one final time. 'If it suits me, I'll sell.'

'Eighty is the last price, take or leave it.'

'Done,' exclaims Babloo, at once. 'But I want all cash, and now.'

As the jeweller walks to his safe to get the cash, Babloo turns to his friend, 'Remember, Bhaiya, you laugh when I would say, I can sell my family jewellery for you. See, I've done it.'

Shivam, who is already feeling guilty, feels even more so and his face falls.

'Find and marry your Aaina now, Bhaiya,' says his friend, his face shining.

'Forget Aaina! Right now, I want to marry you instead,' replies Shivam, hugging him.

Laughing, both leave the shop. Babloo is singing, for he has solved the problem that was gnawing at his mind since morning—dirhams! *Foreign currency is what they had forgotten to buy.* The ticket, passport and visa fees have gobbled up all of the advance money. Shivam too is broke after selling his shop and paying the house rent. He can't send his friend to Dubai with empty pockets, so the jewels. Babloo is sure he won't love his wife more if she adorns all her jewellery. It is useless then and he decides to put it to good use.

28

Babloo and his whole family have come to see off Shivam. Shivam is both excited and nervous. He is flying off to a foreign land to look for someone he doesn't know the address of . . . leaving behind the one person he still has in this world. Babloo busies himself in fetching a trolley and loading it with the one suitcase Shivam is carrying. Rekha stands close to Shivam.

'The whole colony knows about your love story now,' she tells him with stars in her eyes. 'Everyone's now waiting for you to get her here.' She's sad that he's going away, to another girl. In her heart she knows she never had a chance. A part of her is thrilled too to learn what a hero he was, totally filmy.

'If only others could learn to love and go after their woman like you!' That is Rashmi, Babloo's wife. And she looks pointedly at her husband when saying this to Shivam. The sarcasm is not lost on Babloo.

'This is an airport. At least don't suck my blood here!' he hits back. Thank God, she has not found out about the gold set he sold. The day she does, will be his last.

Soon it's time for Shivam to leave. Rekha sidles close to him and whispers in his ear,

'Wear your purple T-shirt when you go to meet her. You look totally like Fardeen Khan. Anyone will flip for you.'

Too many emotions are welling up his throat now. Shivam is unable to speak.

He pats her on the shoulder.

Rekha is in tears. 'I wish my eyes were blue too,' she blurts out, unable to hold back.

He hugs her then.

He looks around for Babloo. But the bugger has been avoiding him since the time they reached the airport. Even now he is walking away from them, towards the cab. Shivam runs after him leaving his baggage trolley, only to be summoned back by a cop who blasts him for leaving his luggage unattended.

Babloo watches him from afar . . . he does not want to break down. Not before Shivam. There will be time for this later. Shivam leaves then. Pushing his trolley towards a whole new world. Seeking a face from the past. It takes him a while to reach his seat on board the aircraft after completing his visa and customs formalities.

'Excuse me . . . 16 A,' he says to a woman as he reaches his seat. The woman in seat 16 B squashes her legs to the side to allow him more space for passage. Shivam squeezes in, careful to avoid touching her knee that is still jutting out a bit. But he is happy it is a window seat.

He looks out the window at the massive wing before him and the airport personnel below on the tarmac. Take-off is exciting for it's his first time on an aeroplane. Soon they are airborne and the buildings below disappear quickly from view. Feeling bereft, he sinks back in his seat and shuts his eyes.

It has not been a month since her kurti found its way back to him. And look where it is taking him now . . . away from all . . . his boutique . . . and Babloo . . . and life, as he knows it. So much beating he has taken . . . not once . . . not twice . . . thrice in three weeks. And he, a body-builder. What more will you make me do . . .

'Aaina!' he sighs out loud, his eyes still shut.

'It's been ages since someone called me by my name.'

Shivam's eyes fly open the second he hears this.

It's the passenger in the next seat.

She turns to him with a smile that reaches her eyes.

'Hi! You know my name,' she says. 'Yours, I don't know.'

'Shivam,' he says while still trying to understand the irony of the situation. She says she is Aaina and he has found her right after boarding the airplane. *Is . . . God fooling around with him again?*

He stares at her in disbelief. She has a classical face, with prominent, arched brows and a sharp nose. Her hair cascades in bouncy waves to just past the shoulders. She looks very attractive in an azure short-sleeved top with a playful tie-me-up bow. Her eyes . . . black.

They are not blue. Again, he checks. *Not blue. Intense and beautiful . . . but not blue.* Puzzled, he withdraws into silence.

When the welcome drinks come, he declines it, not wanting to shell out on the inconsequential. She takes a glass and sips on orange juice. But she doesn't pay. He's wondering why.

She finds him watching her drink surreptitiously.

'Is it free?' he asks, finally.

She bursts out laughing at this, spurting some juice on her pants. A sprinkling on his too.

For some reason, he doesn't mind it.

'It this your first time?' she asks, grabbing some tissues to wipe her clothes. He nods as she hands over one to him too, along with an apology.

'I wasn't laughing at you . . . I'm sorry'

He smiles weakly.

'I saw you sneakily eyeing my juice and I thought . . . you want to pop something in it and sedate me.'

'Ya . . . you should be careful, I am a beast.'

Laughing, she rings the call bell above to order a drink for him.

'Here . . . orange and pineapple . . . two glasses for you,' she says when the tray arrives.

'Do I look starved?' he asks.

'For attention, maybe,' she replies, with a twinkle in her eye.

Two glasses of juice later, he is more in the mood to talk.

'So why does no one call you by your name?'

'Cause no one remembers it . . . my original name, I mean.'

'Parents?'

'It's different when you're adopted,' she says.

That silences him. He can feel her pain in her words. And, yes, pain is something he knows . . . and well understands.

After a minute, she picks up the thread of the conversation again.

'They were a British couple living in Hyderabad. I was barely five when they got me. And the Indian maid they had, she kept calling me Arzoo . . . not Aaina.'

Shivam does not know how to comfort her.

'Aaina, I am, I told her . . . but no one was listening. Cause my new dad . . . he died too . . . after just a month of having adopted me.'

Shivam stares open-mouthed.

'Accident,' she explains. 'This hit my new mom so bad, she left India for good, taking Arzoo with her.'

There's an onboard announcement that lunch is being served.

'So I became Arzoo,' she says, 'forgetting in time . . . that I was ever Aaina.'

'Till I reminded . . . and pained you again.'

'You gave me a chance to be Aaina again,' she returns with a smile.

As the meal trays arrive, both of them get down to the business of eating.

'Tell me your story,' she orders when digging into a spoonful of dessert.

'There's nothing to tell.'

'Aaina . . . where does that fit?'

Shivam puts down his spoon and looks at her.

'What she is to me, I don't know . . . where she is today, don't know . . . all I know is, it's Aaina that I live for,' he says in one breath.

The power of his words silences her.

She doesn't need to hear his full story. Pain, she gathers, is at the heart of it. The pain of separation. And it is this that connects both of them. Making them one in that air journey of a few hours.

'Wow, we're in the same line,' exclaims Arzoo, when he tells her how he entered the tailoring business, following his passion.

'I source ethnic wear for South Asians in London,' she says. 'That's what got me to India . . . and Dubai now.'

The airhostess, there to serve coffee, finds them deep in a discussion about textiles and layered clothing styles.

'Expats there are caught between being Asian and doing the English thing. All the time they feel they're being judged, especially for their clothing,' laments Arzoo. 'So tough it gets at times to choose for them.'

'Layering might work,' suggests Shivam.

'Layering is mostly about temperature control,' she points out.

'Why,' contradicts Shivam. 'It's our choice how we layer.'

Her face says she does not get it.

'How about something modern and trendy . . . and layering it with something more traditional?' he elaborates. 'Like your two-piece nighties.'

She is bowled over by the simplicity of his idea.

Soon they announce descent. They have chatted for the entire three and a half hours but their journey together is far from over.

She gives him her card. 'We could be a team, I think,' she tells him as they collect their baggage and move towards immigration. 'You supplying me clothes, I mean,' she adds, seeing his face frown in question.

'Yes . . . if I get back okay . . . and my designing works for your clients.'

'So . . . ' she holds out her hand . . . in friendship and goodbye.

'Take care, Arzoo,' he says, taking her hand firmly in his.

'Aaina . . . Say it . . . take care, Aaina.'

'Arzoo,' he repeats the name, unable to call another person by that name.

She gulps with the hope that he will. But the words slip out nonetheless. 'I'll pray you get your Aaina, and I know you will. But, if God wills otherwise, this Aaina could be there . . . waiting for you. Look her up.'

He gathers her in a hug. Only to be pushed away.

'Don't. It's Dubai, not Delhi.'

Yes, he realizes as he takes in the Arab stamp all around him. It's a whole new world and culture, one that he will have to negotiate with care, alone. Even Arzoo is gone, breezing out of Immigration and his life. Standing in queue, he waits for what life will bring next.

29

Shankar's brother accosts the new arrival from behind him as Shivam turns his trolley first left, then right, hunting for the Rolex signboard Shankar said Ravi would be standing under.

'I've been waiting for nearly an hour,' grumbles the cook's brother.

Shivam had not expected this. Ravi, in Delhi, had been polite and thankful. This Dubai version would not be easy to put up with.

'I kept one cab waiting and then it finally left.'

'Bhai, Immigration guy had hundred questions . . . what to do! You shouldn't have come.' And Shivam moves ahead with his trolley, not waiting to be guided by this Dubai contact.

'This way, Bhaiya,' Ravi runs after him and apologizes. 'My mood is not so good today,' he says. He bends to take Shivam's luggage from him, stops a taxi and puts it in its hold.

'Have you got your currency for here, dirhams?' he checks, once the two get into the cab.

'A few, I'm carrying what we could manage but I have rupees too if we need more.'

'Dost,' he addresses the taxi driver then. 'Wait for just five minutes I will get his money exchanged . . . super fast, like a rocket.'

'Arrey, not now,' protests Shivam. 'Will exchange when needed.'

But Ravi has his way. He gets fifty thousand rupees converted at the airport money exchange counter.

'Here,' he counts the exchange and hands it over to Shivam, save for one note. 'I'm taking a thousand,' he informs Shivam. 'Don't mind, Bhaiya . . . I too am struggling right now.'

Shivam puts a hand on the chef's shoulder to let him know it's okay, he understands.

Once the note enters his pocket, Ravi turns more helpful. 'I know many agents here. You will get a job immediately . . . don't worry. I'll take you to them . . . Permit, etc., they will manage everything.'

Shivam just nods. Ravi has been chattering all along but Shivam is listening with only half his mind. The city of gold whizzing past his window is so dazzling that he forgets to blink. Gleaming highways stretch in front of them endlessly. On their sides is skyscraper after skyscraper sticking out of an otherwise empty landscape. He is stunned to see each building designed uniquely. A Rolls-Royce zaps past them. A youngster in a Ferrari overtakes them next. It looks like luxury cars are the norm here. Cars and more cars, and buildings all around crowd the picture. Yet, the place looks dead. Almost a ghost town! For people, it strikes him, he barely sees any.

'Because it's afternoon . . . too hot for people to come out,' explains Ravi.

'Still, not a soul on the road, except in cars.'

'That's the culture here. It's impossible to walk around in this heat.'

'And those who don't have—'

Ravi interrupts him. 'Bhaiya, see, Burj Khalifa!'

Standing tall before them is a huge outlandish structure, jutting out to the skies, proclaiming supremacy over all that lies beneath. The taxi driver slows down to allow the new arrival a better look. It is mind-boggling.

'Tallest in the world it is,' claims Ravi, with pride. 'It took five years to build. It will be opening next month. You'll get to see from the inside.'

Where he will be next month? Shivam doesn't know, so he keeps quiet.

'Jumeirah and Marina . . . then Deira . . . remember,' Ravi instructs the cab driver.

Down the Sheikh Zayed Road, they go past the downtown area, full of malls and office towers. As they cross the business area, the view changes abruptly. Low-rising structures line the road. Lavish residences sit grandly on large, open spaces.

'Resorts and bungalows, mostly,' comments Ravi.

As they turn a corner, they come upon the sea . . . It seems to appear out of nowhere, startling the newcomer. Shivam rubs his eyes in disbelief because he can see palm-shaped islands floating on it, beautiful and logic-defying . . . .

'Palm Jumeirah,' says Ravi. 'World's largest man-made island.'

'Everything's so excessive here, so showy and dramatic . . .'

'It's in your eyes . . . As you see it . . . it becomes,' says the cab driver. 'I see tourists go "wow–wow" over it . . . some even irritated by it.'

He was right. Shivam was in no frame of mind to appreciate the extravagant marvels of man in this desert country. Otherwise, maybe, he too would've oohed and aahed over it. As for Babloo, he would gape, mouth open . . . this he was sure of. Reminded of his friend, Shivam twists restlessly in his seat. He asks Ravi, 'How far is your place? . . . Will it take long?'

'Half hour . . . maybe, one, depends . . . ' Ravi replies, gazing out of the window, enjoying the drive and the music on his headphones.

'Do you still want me to take Marina?' asks the driver, checking again.

Ravi responds irritably, 'Why are you asking me again and again. I told you at the airport.'

'Your friend doesn't seem to want any more sightseeing, so I thought you might want to go straight.'

'Sightseeing?' Shivam turns to Ravi, incredulously.

'Forget, Marina . . . Deira straight,' barks Ravi to the driver. 'Bhaiya,' he defends himself to Shivam, 'I thought you'll want to have a look of the city since this is your first time here and we won't take a taxi every day, so I . . . '

Shivam is not amused. *Shankar's brother seems too cunning . . . he'll need to be careful. He can't blow his dirhams like this . . . Babloo has sold everything for them.* Fifteen minutes of silent driving later, they reach the Deira apartment. Ravi jumps out and pulls Shivam's suitcase from the back and starts dragging it in, leaving Shivam to settle the taxi fare. As the lift shoots up to the fourteenth floor, Shivam wonders how the hell he will adjust with this chef who expects him to cough up dirhams every hour.

* * *

Four faces surround him as Shivam opens his suitcase. They are all Ravi's flatmates, living together in this one-bedroom, one hall–kitchen apartment.

We will be nearly half a dozen here now! And for this micro space, the smart-ass has made him shell out 1000 dirhams! Had it been India, with just one whack, he would've sent the swine flying back to his brother's dhaba.

Swallowing his indignation, Shivam takes out the packets Ravi's brother has sent for him.

'Here, take this zeera. Shankar has sent it for you.'

Ravi walks over to take the packet. He holds it up to his nose and breathes in deeply, inhaling its aroma.

'Not zeera . . . shahzeera,' he corrects Shivam.

'Ah! Now we'll get that biryani,' exclaims the tallest of the flatmates, seeing Shivam pass on the turmeric and the garam masala packets too. 'All your spices have come.'

By evening, the promised biryani has been made. All six of them sit in a circle polishing it off with great relish.

'It's to die for,' declares the tall man, as he ladles a second helping for himself.

'Bhaiya, he's Nawab,' Ravi introduces him. 'By name . . . and by work.'

Everyone laughs.

Ravi goes on to explain, 'He works at the British Embassy as an office boy. The whole day he sits yawning in an AC room. Even for tea–coffee, English sahib all get up and help themselves while this Nawab just sits and gets fat.'

Nawab smiles and pats his tummy.

'And this is Ramendu,' Ravi points out the man sitting opposite Shivam. 'He's head plumber in a sanitary company.'

Shivam nods.

'He's Ketan. I'm Navin.' The last two introduce themselves, not waiting for Ravi to do the honours.

'Both of us are supervisors at a construction site,' adds Navin.

'They are involved in the construction of the Dubai Mall,' Ravi says. 'That Burj Khalifa I showed you? It's there only. Best in Dubai it will be . . . ice skating . . . aquarium . . . dancing fountains! You name it, it will be there.'

'Sounds exciting, but it's not. It is back-breaking to manage all the labour. We're dead by half-shift,' says Navin.

'And any shit that happens . . . we only get hauled up. Not the managers, not the workers.' This was Navin's fellow supervisor, Ketan, adding his two bit.

Shivam nods in understanding. These two were repeating what another person working in Dubai once told him years ago.

Ravi jumps in again to complete the introductions. 'And Shivam's a close friend, like I told you all before. He's come here for a job.'

Shivam frowns at how Ravi presents him. Not a paying tenant, but a friend and a freeloader.

This chef is milking both ways. Fooling him and his flatmates too.

'Till he gets a job, he can look after the house,' adds Ramendu.

'And here's the directory . . . catch,' shouts Nawab, chucking a thick book at him. 'Lists all the placement agents.'

The Dubai Mall-making boys wash off their plates and stand smoking near the window before retiring to their mattress. They keep quiet and to themselves. And that's how they are every day, as Shivam finds out in time. Their heavy workload drains them of all energy and spirit to dream of anything after work hours.

Shivam stations himself and his mattress next to Nawab's and chews his brain on how to go about these placement agencies.

'Face wash and dress neat and go. And don't forget your CV, passport and visa copies. Rest all inshallah.'

Some insight that was in job hunting! Shivam beat his head. Best was to follow his own instinct. As he lies on the mattress that night, looking out the window at the moon and distant stars, he feels could've been anywhere . . . Delhi, Dubai or even Aligarh. The chill of the air conditioner and Nawab's small talk is all that marks this night as different . . . and international.

'This is Dreamland . . . *jannat!*'

'Jannat,' repeats Shivam. 'Then I'll get all that I want?'

'Everything,' replies Nawab.

Shivam smiles, half-asleep even as Nawab drones on.

'Job, money, food, imported stuff . . . yes, everything.'

Shivam shuts his eyes and starts dreaming of a tomorrow full of . . .

'Except a girl, you will get everything here.'

He hears that and he can sleep no more.

Nawab dozes off. So do the four others in the room. Now, Shivam lies quietly, questioning the moon. *Will his journey be in vain?*

30

Shivam short-lists ten placement agencies. Nawab says these are popular with Indians seeking semi-skilled jobs. Shivam stands at the gate of the first one and looks up at the board—*Wadi Jobs*.

'Are you looking for a job?' The receptionist greets Shivam the minute he walks in.

'I'm looking for some information,' replies Shivam.

'Regarding a job, you mean . . . '

'Regarding a girl . . . Aaina . . . she has blue eyes . . .' he starts giving more details that he imagines will help her. 'Did she come here looking for a job?'

The receptionist gives him an angry look.

Shivam rushes to clarify 'No . . . don't misunderstand me. I know her . . . I . . . I mean I knew her, so it's important that I find her. I was just checking if she contacted your agency. I need to know . . . please.'

The receptionist calls the guard on the intercom. Before he can get into trouble with the security, Shivam rushes out. Ravi's many warnings echo in his ears: 'Don't swear, eat or drink in public. No losing your temper when you're out. Even checking someone else's phone is illegal. They could jail you for blinking here. Last year, a guy got deported for being too handsome.' So, for the next placement agency on his list, Shivam changes tack.

'I've got a visitor's visa,' he tells the person manning the counter at *Future Focus*. 'I want a job before it expires. My cousin recommended your agency. She got hired through you two years back. You're the best, she said.'

'Can you do welding?' checks the man at the counter after learning Shivam's qualifications and experience. 'Tailoring doesn't have a chance here as lady tailors are needed for ladies.'

Welding, he declines but he is ready to try other options when they become available. After registering in the jobseeker databank, he turns to go. At the door, he does a U-turn and asks casually, 'That cousin who recommended you . . . I can't connect with her now. Could you check your database once? Maybe, her number changed.'

And the man falls for it.

'Aaina Farooqui . . . Aaina . . . 2001 . . . India . . . ' mumbles the fellow as he scrolls down the company database. He finally declares, 'No Aaina Farooqui.'

'How about just Aaina . . . or Aaina something else?'

The *Future Focus* rep looks annoyed now.

'One last time please see . . . she's the only contact I've got here.'

With a scowl, the man at the counter runs the search again.

'No Aaina,' he confirms after checking. 'You've got the wrong agency.'

'Registering with a different name not possible na'

'This is Dubai, not Delhi,' he almost shouts. Getting up from his chair, he points to the door. His patience for this dubious job seeker has run out.

Shivam walks out happily, having got the information he wanted. This wasn't the agency she had come to. Ticking it off the list, he plans to focus on placement agency number three for the next day. Late that evening, he returns to the apartment—or bedspace, as the locals called this type of one-bedroom-with-balcony lodging, where the bathroom is common for all rooms on that floor. Too tired to chat or eat, he sits in the balcony and watches the rest of his roommates trickle in one by one.

'How did it go?' Nawab asks as soon as he sees him.

'Arrey did you mention you are embassy wallah's contact . . . straight MD post they'll get you . . . like this,' Ramendu snaps his fingers.

'No . . . he took your name,' Nawab counters him. 'And down the drain pipe they were sending him.'

Ravi joins the banter. As do the construction worker twins when they walk in. Filling the bedspace with cheer and laughter at the end of a tiring and sweaty day.

Next day, with the next agency on the list, Shivam goes about it with a manic dedication. And on the third day, he strikes silver, if not gold.

Rustom at *Gulf Workers* is friendly. After fifteen minutes of hedging, Shivam decides to confide he is after Aaina and not a job.

'Let me run a system search,' offers Rustom. 'We'll know if she came here.'

Shivam sits there, holding his breath. No Aaina appears in his search unfortunately.

'What next,' he asks, knowing Rustom will be the right person to seek advice from.

'Look I won't tell you it will be easy but I can tell you where to look,' says Rustom. 'Nurse, teacher or nanny, that's what she will be doing. Female jobs are mostly in this category.'

'Okay . . . so I should check schools and hospitals first?'

'Right. But this is not India,' Rustom warns him. 'It is impossible to walk in and bribe someone here.'

'I'll try. I've got to reach her . . . anyhow.'

Rustom raises his hands in surrender. *Not just blind, love is foolish and impractical as well! No point in arguing.*

'One more favour . . . ' Shivam is hesitant as he asks.

'Shoot.'

'Please share the school and hospital lists where you think the chances of finding her are big.'

'Okay, I'll give you printouts tomorrow.'

Shivam's face falls.

Rustom melts at that. 'Wait! I've got ten minutes to spare, let me see what I can do.'

He manages to sort twelve likely venues and prints them out, before wrapping up for the day.

Shivam is almost in tears. This is so unexpected he does not know how to thank Rustom. He needn't because as they step out of the office together, Rustom grips his new-found friend by the shoulder. 'Look, I've been so busy making money here that I never thought about girls. I realize now that my life is quite empty,' he confesses. 'I don't want yours to be like mine. Go find her!'

Clutching onto the two sheets from Rustom, Shivam trudges back to the apartment, his heart more hopeful.

Come morning, dreams tend to disperse and Shivam's goal too gets distant. He does not get entry into even one school. Even at the hospitals they ask him a hundred questions at the gate.

'Do you have a health card?'

'I'm a tourist, not a local,' he says.

'Okay, then show your passport.'

When he tells them it's not in his pocket right now, they ask him to leave. His passport is locked in Ravi's drawer and cannot be retrieved until night. So he pleads with the guards. He stands there in the sun for hours, hoping to melt their hearts or sneak in. Nothing works. But a European coming to the same hospital—touted as the AIIMS of Dubai—simply walks through, no questions asked.

'We're the wrong E,' Nawab explains to him that night. 'Dubai dances to Emirati or European tune. Expats like us don't exist. We're imported only for donkey-work.'

'Manager or plumber . . . you will always be second class. Always,' says Ramendu, sharing his own experience.

Shivam sighs. The Dubai sheen is wearing off even before it has come on. Every night he sinks into a dreamless sleep, waking only to the construction supervisors' morning alarm.

The next day, he leaves early, but not before taking his passport from Ravi. Dubai Healthcare City is the target. Rustom from *Gulf Workers* suggested he tried there first. It turns out to be a huge complex, with most modern and premium healthcare facilities across specialities under one roof. 'Which way to Emergency?' he asks, holding the passport in his hand. The security guard, in uniform, points to the left and lets him pass.

Once inside, Shivam crawls through one hospital building to the other, missing no floor or department. Enquiring about her at every nursing station. 'Aaina, I'm looking for. Aaina from India . . . she came to work here . . . two years back.' Four hours go by and he covers five buildings but there is no trace of Aaina yet. Only the dental medicentre is left now. The receptionist in the lobby of the Al-Habib Medicentre stops him from taking the lift.

'Have you got an appointment, sir?'

'No. I just need a . . . ' His mobile rings just then. It is Babloo.

'Camel ride going okay?' his friend quips.

'I've come to Dubai Medicity.'

'What! Are you sick? What happened . . . tell me . . . what happened?'

Shivam almost has to scream to shut him up. 'I'm fine. Chill. I am.'

Unconvinced, Babloo argues, 'You are hiding something, Bhaiya. I know you are.'

Shivam steps out of the medicentre to hear Babloo more clearly. Also, he needs to shout the fellow down so Babloo doesn't keep singing like this and eat up whatever balance is left on his card.

'*Chup be*! I'm telling you na I'm okay. Should I repeat in Chinese? Now listen. I came here for her. Not me.'

'Ohhh!'

'The whole day has gone, I got nothing. I've checked six hospitals, all everyone does is nod their head and say "don't know" or "don't have time". I'm going mad.'

'Bhaiya, don't give up. We have to find her.'

'I know. But I don't know where to look now.'

'Bhaiya, think again . . . what did Rustom say . . . all places she could be . . . think . . . '

'Babloo . . . schools, hospitals, is what he said.'

'And?'

'And chances are, she's a nanny. But I can't invade homes asking "Do you know Aaina? She came from India two years back. Is she your nanny? I'm hunting the whole world for her." I can't do that na?'

'Don't do drama, Bhaiya . . . you will . . . '

'She's my nanny.' Shivam turns with the speed of lightning, the phone slipping from his hand. A woman is standing right behind him. She is the one who has spoken.

'You . . . you know Aaina?' He stammers.

'Yes. She supervises my kids. My husband got her from Delhi a couple of years back.'

Shivam is almost in tears as he bends to pick up his phone. *Just when he was about to break . . . she had come, an angel sent to keep him going.* Hands folded, he requests Aaina's contact details. 'She's all I've got.'

'Come home and meet her. She'll be happy to see you . . . someone from home after so long.'

And soon they are driving away, him in the front seat, next to the driver and Madam at the back, on her phone.

'She was a surprise from my husband so that I can be freer,' she says, gushing, in between her calls.

He wants to ask her so much . . . *Is she fine? Is she liking Dubai? Does she speak of home . . . of things that happened . . . things she left behind . . . of people . . . of him . . .*

He hopes she is not overworked. But he does not have the guts to ask the madam so many questions. Also, she does not have the time. She is busy on her phone for most of the ride.

It is taking an eternity to reach where these people live. Shivam drums his fingers on the glove box, restlessly. Thirty minutes later, the car slides into the driveway of a huge mansion. Shivam looks around as he gets down.

These people are rich. Filthy rich. Loaded! They must have taken good care of her.

He thanks God for this blessing. Though he's not religious, he has done that twice already today. First, for the angel who had spoken to him . . . and second, now.

'You wait here . . . in the foyer, I'll send her.'

Shivam waits, his heart racing, pulse overtaking. His mind flits from yesterday to tomorrow, dwelling in moments in which she will be with him.

'Beta, come close . . . my eyesight is dimming now.'

Putting his daydream on pause, Shivam walks up to the woman who summons him in the hallway.

Instead of taking him to Aaina, she calls him closer. She takes his face in her wizened hands. She had rough and wrinkled but strong hands. She examines him up-close. Like a microbe, he allows himself to be peered at through those aged lenses.

'Are you Durgesh's son?' Her question baffles him and he draws away.

'I want to meet Aaina, Auntyji.'

She laughs. A cackle that rises in her chest, gets high-pitched, and makes her rock. It takes her almost a minute to settle down.

'It's been ages since I've heard that.'

Shivam stands like a statue, not knowing what to say or think. Her declaration makes no sense to him. *But wait, a corner of his brain wakes up. Where had he heard that line last, recently? Yes, on the flight. Arzoo . . . she had declared the same thing when he took Aaina's name . . . what does that mean?*

He fights it, not ready to accept what is staring him in the face.

'You are Aaina?' He finally manages to breathe out those words.

She gathers him in a hug, fondling his head, petting his hair.

'Durgesh's son, you are . . . true copy,' she tells him, her voice going emotional. 'He used to tease me so.'

Shivam keeps his mouth shut. He allows her to hug and pet him. He sits by her for half an hour and listens to her tales of Agra, where she used to stay with her mother who died fifteen years ago. Durgesh was their neighbour and her soul mate. A decade and a half later, she is overjoyed by this surprise visit from Shivam, who she takes to be her neighbour's son. Shivam lets her think that.

Trudging back to the bedspace at night, he does not feel as empty as he should. At least he has made one Aaina happy.

31

Even before the sun, he is up. There is this time bomb ticking in his head, reminding him that the days in his one-month visa are fast running out. So are the dirhams. *Just fifteen days more, he will have to find her quickly. But where?* He stands by the window and looks out. Where to go next? Schools, hospitals, agencies . . . none has gotten him any nearer to his goal. Where then? And the answer literally stares back at him.

See You at the Dubai Shopping Festival!
Unbeatable Deals! Big Entertainment! Even Bigger Prizes!
Come, Shop, Eat, Enjoy. Win Millions of AED!
*City Centre Deira *Mall of the Emirates *Ibn Battuta Mall

The huge hoarding is promising the moon. *Should he? Dubai is all about malls and he hasn't looked for her in any of them. How could he not have!*

One of the construction supervisors joins him at the window. He can't believe it when Shivam asks him which mall to go to first.

'You have not been to any?' he asks incredulously like he has committed a crime by not visiting the city's shopping heavens. Perhaps, he has. For Dubai is about malls and the great deals and brands you get in them. Every highway here seems to end in a mall. All the top hotels have come up in them. So have the cinemas and restaurants.

'But you've been here for fifteen days!' Ketan says.

'He's not come here to shop.' Ravi rises to Shivam's defence.

'Accha, you go to malls to shop?' Ketan asks Ravi. 'All those Saturdays you while away there . . . you are shopping, right?'

Ravi is caught. 'I . . . I do timepass.'

Shivam is confused now. *Should he try the malls or will it be just timepass?*

Ketan clears the air. 'We all go to pass time . . . but we go. Mall is the park here,' he explains to Shivam. 'Everyone does.'

'Your workers can't,' points out Ravi. 'Mall security won't let them in, you know.'

'Forget them . . . that's labour class . . . their life is different. We can't compare.'

'So, expats . . . they all come there?' Shivam checks with him again.

'That's the only outlet we've got,' replies Ketan. 'Low income-high income, old-young, all flock to this air-conditioned space in their off-time.'

'Most times, we are only leching,' Ravi confesses.

'Not at girls,' Ketan is quick to clarify.

'At people, mostly. How they walk, dress and show-off. Making an ass of themselves . . . all that.'

'And girls . . . they come there . . . in free time?'

Ketan jumps in to warn him. 'Don't go after girls here. Not in malls . . . not anywhere.'

Ravi adds, 'Which jail they chuck you . . . you won't know . . . not till your coffin comes.'

'I was just asking . . .'

Ketan has to go for his bath. Ravi continues dispensing his gyan on expat girls.

'Malls are full of them,' he says. 'Salesgirls in stores. At information counters. Food courts. You find them everywhere. Most are Bangladeshis and Filipinas. Indians, also. But . . . but you don't make the first move.' He pauses. 'No move, you make.'

Shivam pats Ravi's shoulder to reassure him. Then, seeing Ketan come out, he moves to get ready.

'Start with Deira City Centre,' Ketan says.

'Then Ibn Battuta,' adds Navin. 'And Mall of the Emirates, last.'

He hops in the cab with Ketan and Navin. They'll drop him at the Deira City Centre on their way. He'll save some dirhams this way.

Brimming with hope, he enters the vast, glitzy mall and is greeted by one global brand after another. Marble flooring, tinted glass walls and chilled air-conditioning make the sweltering sun outside non-existent. Escalators run up and down across the mall space. And he sees hundreds . . . no, thousands . . . of shoppers, visitors and timepass characters riding them. Shivam has not seen half as many people in the whole of Dubai since he arrived. Not a soul does he see on the streets, just cars and more cars flitting by. It is only in schools, hospitals and agencies that he comes across people walking. As for Emirati, he has not seen one outside the airport. It's expats and more expats, flooding all places.

'The one stamping your passport could be the only one you get to see,' Nawab had said. 'Emiratis keep to themselves, mingling a little and, that too, mostly with the Whites or expats they do business with.'

Here, in the mall, he sees a couple of cool white robes floating about on the second floor. Then another, inside a luxury watch brand store, making up his mind about a Tag Heuer watch, the store manager holds up for him.

Their women folk strut around in high heels, clutching shopping bags in their bejewelled hands, some in hijab, some with face uncovered. *But his Aaina is nowhere.* In all the black burqas gliding about, or the scarfed beauties passing him by, not one is Aaina.

He scouts all three floors of the Deira City Centre . . . five to six times . . . From the salesgirls in the stores to those manning the cafes and info booths on every floor, he searches every face and scans every woman who comes to shop as well as those accompanying their mistress.

Shivam would know her, hijab or no hijab. All those hours of watching from that tank in her school playground . . . he is a pro where she is concerned. *Twenty feet away, he can tell if it's her, just by her shape, the way she moves, how she carries herself. Up close, her voice, her smell, yes, he knows that too. And her eyes, of course, they are a dead giveaway. He can never mistake her with another. Never.*

So he looks for her. Up and down the mall. Again. And again. Peering into every shop, restaurant and aisle. He sees Indians crowding the electronic stores . . . and the Carrefour supermarket. He checks these points every hour, hoping the next black-haired girl who walks in there has blue eyes too. But dreams are dreams. At midnight, when the festive mall downs its shutters and says goodbye to everyone, he returns to his bedspace.

Next day, it's the turn of the Ibn Battuta Mall.

'It will whack you hollow,' warns Ravi. 'I'm sure you've never seen anything like it.'

So Shivam goes prepared to be inundated with Dubai excesses . . . it seems to be the culture here. Three domes poke out of a grey, a cemented roof that stretches on and on . . . as far as he can see. The Deira City Centre was huge. This looks ten times its size. Shivam sighs. *How will he find her in this gargantuan monster of a place!*

He calls Rustom.

'You're at the right place,' Rustom tells him. 'They've got live shows there, check out the timings. Look out for her at the show. Some floor you might find her . . . by the railing . . . enjoying the event below.'

Before he disconnects, Rustom adds, 'Security is very strict . . . keep your distance. One guard you annoy, you'll rot in jail forever. No one will hear your version.'

Warned, Shivam steps in gingerly and goes past the army of security. He is alert and checks the huge flow of people and their bags.

Ravi is right! It is like a different world inside here! Ibn Battuta's world! It celebrates all the places the medieval explorer has been to—India, China, Andalusia . . . All these places have come alive once more in this mall, in its themed courts and their distinct architecture and décor. Like a tourist, Shivam stands marvelling at this wonderland.

His cell phone rings. 'Bhaiya, where you lost?' Babloo knows just when to catch him, almost like they have been wired together.

'Babloo, this mall I'm at, it's like I've gone back hundreds of years . . . '

'*Arrey,* Bhaiya . . . you are after Aaina's grandma now . . . huh!' Happily they go on and on, connecting with each other over thousands of miles across the world. Shivam needs this, a voice he knows. A person of his own. Everything else is unfamiliar in this Arab land.

'Focus . . . Bhaiya, focus on your girl,' teases Babloo.

'And you on your Chaddhaji,' he retorts.

His friend has been ribbing him but suddenly goes serious. 'Next week, I'll have to leave for London.'

'What! Why you didn't tell me before!' Shivam curses, chiding himself for not remembering. The departure was imminent, he should've realized. He is so caught up in his own life he has not even asked Babloo how things are going at his end.

'I would've called before the flight,' Babloo reassures him.

'You would. For tips, saale.'

'Yes, for that too,' Babloo agrees, laughing. 'What's eating me Bhaiya is . . . I won't be here when you come back.'

Shivam blanks out as he realizes what this means. And what Babloo means to him—he is Shivam's solitary pillar.

'It's okay,' he says. 'Those White girls won't let you stick around for long. Two return tickets they'll book for you and your lousy voice even before Chaddhaji *ka* show ends.'

Three women in burqas walk by him just then. One of them reminds Shivam of someone and he disconnects the phone abruptly. He chases her to the next court where he accidentally bumps into a large Chinese junk boat displayed in the middle. His foot gets stuck in the yawning hole on one side of its wooden body. There's a loud thud as he falls, the boat toppling along with him to the marble floor.

Everyone around him stops. As do the burqa-clad women. Security rushes in to check what has happened. The woman who feels familiar also steps closer for a better look. Instead of tending to his foot, his back, and the side of him that hurt from hitting the floor, Shivam is more concerned about the colour of her . . . eyes. They *are brown. Also, she's shorter. Yes, about three inches less. Even with her heels she doesn't reach up to Aaina's height.*

'F . . .' he curses, but stops himself just in time. There's security and people all around him. And cussing is banned in Dubai.

'Definitely not in public,' Ravi has drilled that into him time and again.

Two rounds of questioning follow—he apologizes for being a selfie-crazy tourist and a hazard to Dubai's priceless art pieces—before he is let off by the security. Every muscle on his left side aches as he roams the mall again. *Aaina, you're taking a toll on my skeletal system!*

Complaining to his lady-love as usual fetches no answers or solutions. Again, he goes marching in and out of all the high-fashion footwear, clothing and accessory brand stores, his eyes on the female retail executives working there—straightening clothes, handling receipts, attending to customers. He hopes to find a familiar face in them.

Half the day goes by, yet he has not managed to cover even half the mall. Every bit of him aches like it will fall off if he does not sit down right away. So he lumbers up to the life-size elephant clock occupying one corner of the India-themed courtyard and flops on the tiny marble ledge he spies behind it. Eyes shut, he breathes in deep, resting his back against the board there, happy to have found this hidden corner in the crowded mall.

God, like you found me this ledge . . . get me my girl too . . . before I break. He sits praying.

Next instant, she falls, plop, on his lap. His eyes snap open, body jerking to attention at this sudden weight.

'What the . . . '

She puts a hand on his lips and as their eyes lock, he falls silent.

32

Her eyes, large, scared and beseeching. Her slim body quashing against his. He almost falls . . . and regains his balance just in time to hold her and stop her from slipping to the floor.

'Hide me,' she pleads with him as someone shouts in the distance.

The two of them sit on the tiny ledge. She is squeezing close to him so not an inch of her is visible to the world that exists on the other side of the elephant.

Two . . . three . . . five . . . ten minutes pass in this way. With both of them hidden from the world by the huge Indian showpiece.

'Turquoise blue . . . do you see my mistress in turquoise blue?' she asks him, trembling as she points to the world she is hiding from. 'She is fat, has big hoop earrings and two kids,' she adds.

Shivam cranes his neck to look but doesn't find her in the milling crowd. As he makes an effort to get up and move, she pulls him down again.

'Don't go,' she begs. 'Please. Save me from them. I've been a prisoner for more than two years.' And her big, brown eyes fill up with tears. 'They don't let me call home, not even once. They just make me work and work till I drop dead on the bed at night. My body, it hurts . . . still she abuses me . . . calls me slow.'

Shivam is appalled. 'Why you didn't just quit and go?'

'They've taken my passport.'

'Oh! How will you manage then . . . you still don't have it?'

'I don't know . . . I'll die on the road but I won't go back to her.'

He helps her sneak out of the mall. When she's safe from her mistress in turquoise, he hands over half of the last few dirhams he has. She needs them more than him. The brown-eyed girl dispatched, Shivam returns to resume his hunt for his blue-eyed girl. From Debenhams to H&M, Yas Perfumes to Arabian Oud, he roams every outlet and inch of the huge Ibn Battuta Mall that day, the next day, and the day after that too. He comes across scores of people but not her.

Back at the apartment, he is chopping vegetables with Ramendu while Nawab is on his computer.

'Oye, Nawab!' shouts Ramendu. 'Leave your Facebook. Come and cook. Your turn today.'

'Yaar, give ten minutes just . . . One old friend of mine, I came to know she's here . . . in Dubai. Looking for her only.'

Shivam's antennae go up. He chucks the vegetables he is chopping and scampers up to Nawab. 'You can find people on computer too?'

'Everything's on Google, Facebook now. You should only know how to look.'

'Will you find one girl for me?' Shivam asks tentatively.

'At your service, Romeo,' replies Nawab with a mock bow and a naughty smile. 'Just shoot her name. Fast.'

'Aaina.'

Nawab types *Aaina* and a list of Aainas come up on the screen. They look for the ones in Dubai. Shivam checks each profile carefully.

Meanwhile, Ramendu is going mad. First, Nawab and now Shivam have this Facebook bug.

'I'm only cooking for myself,' he says.

'Just two more minutes,' begs Nawab. 'Think of my tummy.'

In all those Aainas, Shivam can't find that one Aaina who is his . . .

'Maybe, she's not on the net yet,' says Nawab, shutting the computer.

Online. Offline. She seems to be nowhere. Only in his dreams, she comes. Beckoning. Teasing him to find her. Catch her. Like he tried to do at kho kho, years ago. And lost. No . . . he couldn't afford to lose this time.

So he travels to Shaykh Zayed Road the next morning. He enters the Mall of the Emirates. This mall is said to have everything a human may desire. Even a ski slope with snow and pine trees has been erected in a mammoth freezer, defying the sweltering Gulf heat. It is considered the grandest of all malls. But by now, all malls look the same to Shivam. Sprawling marble spaces with shiny floors and bright lighting, amidst which twinkle the same global brands . . . day after day.

Come evening, the crowd of visitors surges; they come in droves for the live shows. Shivam grows restless. This place has everything . . . everything except what he really wants. Up and down the floors he goes, scanning every person walking by. *Another day will end with nothing in his hand.* Shivam drums his fingers impatiently on the escalator handrail as he climbs up to the third floor.

And then . . . up the same moving railing, his gaze falls on a charm bracelet encircling a tiny wrist that rests on the handrail.

It's the same bracelet he gave her . . . tied it around her wrist as she left him with tears . . . going with Babloo . . . her last moment with him . . .

'Aaina!' He screams as she reaches the third floor and steps off. He tries to rush up but can't. So many women are before him on the escalator. They block his way. In a few seconds, she becomes invisible again. He goes crazy. He runs around, looking for that figure in pink, sporting his bracelet. Yes, it is his bracelet. He is sure. As sure as he has been of anything, ever. It is not just the bracelet, he also senses it is her. Yes, he can.

But the floor seems to have eaten her up. Nowhere can he spot her. There are too many shops and more and more people keep coming. Even the food courts are on this floor. He goes round and round, his mind also spinning, as he keeps racing to the escalators and back to see if she took them again.

An hour later, when he has checked the food court for the thirteenth time, a guard walks up to him.

'My girl's picture fell from my wallet . . . it was the only one I had.'

The guard buys his excuse but tells him to be careful. 'In fact, forget about it,' he says. 'While looking,' he warns Shivam, 'if you bump into anyone, you'll be in deep, deep trouble.'

Sick of going in circles, Shivam leaves the third floor. She is gone. Even if she was there, he knows he won't find her now. It is as if the floor has swallowed her up.

He goes down to the ground floor, away from the performances being staged. They don't interest him. The music has gone from his life. He lingers by the mall entrance, hoping to catch her on her way out.

Till midnight, he stays put. Thousands of women walk past the gates. Not one wrist sports his bracelet though.

33

He has ten more days. Seven, if he plans considering Babloo's departure for London,

'Bhaiya, I want you here before I go,' he tells him.

'Am I your girlfriend that you'll kiss goodbye?' Shivam asks, teasing.

'You know I'll be more confident if you are there,' insists Babloo. This is his first flight too.

'I also want to Babloo . . . '

'Arrey, I'm joking Bhaiya.' Babloo changes tack. He doesn't want his friend to feel guilty about not making it back on time. 'So busy I'll be practising, I won't have time to meet you. Chaddhaji is dancing on my head all the time.'

Shivam returns to the Mall of the Emirates the next day. But his heart is heavy and mind, restless. *Is he chasing a mirage in the desert? He has a few more days . . . and very few dirhams left to find out.*

He walks the millions of square feet of the mall, treading places she trod yesterday. He strolls past Louis Vuitton and Burberry. DKNY and Bvlgari. Not forgetting the Apple store. The place is teeming with people, same as yesterday. Shopping seems to be the national pastime here. He feels he has become a camel, for how much he has been walking in this desert nation. His feet are killing him. His head throbs and his throat is parched.

So he splurges this one time. He buys himself a small cup of grossly overcharged coffee. As he stands sipping it and watching the world flit by, he picks a fight with God. *Even you are playing games with me now! First, you dump the wrong woman in my lap. Then my girl comes and goes in a blink. Go on . . . test me . . . have your fun. But if I lose . . . remember, you lose too . . .*

A Bangladeshi grabbing coffee alongside has been watching him pick bones silently.

'Dubai has this effect on people,' he says sagely. 'You start talking to yourself.'

Shivam just nods.

The man is in a talkative mood. He says he is a sales guy at this mall.

'Do you like it here?' asks Shivam, thinking about the Filipina nanny who landed on his lap while trying to escape her mistress.

'It was okay at first,' replies the man, cautiously, lowering his voice. 'But after a time . . . you start feeling trapped.'

'Trapped,' echoes Shivam. That's exactly what the escaped nanny said. He shares her escapade with this newfound Bangla friend.

'That is nothing new. It happens all the time here in parks and malls and parties. With passports confiscated, these girls have no choice, they have to either run away or stay slaves,' he tells him. 'But you shouldn't get involved . . . It's dicey here, with the law.'

'Yes, but I couldn't have just let her be.'

'You have to here,' maintains the Bangla salesman. 'You learn not to see what you see.'

Shivam's face wrinkles up as he does not follow what the man is trying to say.

'Okay, ten more minutes I've got . . . come, I'll show you something.' He takes him into the basement parking. The fourth basement . . . is the lowest level, where car owners are reluctant to park. It is a massive, empty space, all lit-up, but abandoned. No visitor cars here. There is just one uniformed man near the electronic barrier. Shivam panics for a second. He should've thought twice before coming down here with this stranger.

'See that car,' the Bangla salesman points to a Range Rover standing in the far corner.

'Yes,' mutters Shivam, looking at the super-luxury vehicle parked in the distance.

'Look inside,' orders his guide. 'There's a boy in there . . . in the rear.'

He is right. Shivam can make out the faint outline of someone half-sitting, half-lying on the backseat.

'So claustrophobic it must be to wait in here,' observes Shivam.

'He lives here.'

'What!'

Shivam can't believe this. *How can one anyone live here . . . in the underground? And why should they . . . in a car . . . alone?*

'That's Dubai for you.'

The expat's words take his mind back to the Filipino nanny.

'Are they like this with all their staff here?' he asks.

'He's not staff. He owns it,' says the Bangladeshi. 'Crazy partying lifestyle landed his parents in debt . . . then jail. So the fifteen-year-old now lives here . . . in their car . . . till parents finish their sentence and manage to buy tickets to fly them out.'

Stunned, Shivam simply stands, staring. Only when they're in the lift going up again does he regain his voice to ask, 'The security . . . do they say nothing?'

'They understand . . . and look the other way.'

After the salesman returns to his duty, Shivam does not have the stamina to wander the mall any more. What he's seen in the parking lot has drained him. He goes back to the apartment, feeling hopeless and low. This is not a country where he will get what he wants. It has only illusions to offer. He has reached home early and fishes for the keys in his pocket.

No one will be back yet. Good. He'll get some time to himself. To think. Plan the next move. Next move . . . is there one?

He is surprised to see Ravi inside, lying on the couch. *Why is the cook not in the restaurant?* Just as he opens his mouth to ask, he remembers the Bangladeshi's advice . . . to not see . . . and let be. He stays quiet and sits in the balcony, gazing out.

Ravi follows him there half an hour later. Slowly, in bits, it all comes stuttering out.

'Job is gone . . . pay too they cut and gave.' He is almost paralysed with embarrassment as he unburdens himself. 'Shankar Bhaiya . . . what will I tell him now? I can't stay here like this. And I can't go back also. He's buying a plot in Punjab. There will be huge loans. And his pride . . . Bhaiya has told everyone his brother is now a big shot in Dubai.'

Shivam does not interrupt him. He lets it all flow out. It needs to. Too much is simmering in the cook's chest. Feeling lighter, Ravi falls quiet. And the two sit there for some time, simply gazing at the skyline.

'Go back home,' Shivam finally bursts out. 'Before Shankar Bhaiya buys that plot . . . before you get trapped here forever . . . go.'

He narrates the story of the Filipino nanny trying to escape . . . and the plight of the fifteen-year-old surviving in his dad's Range Rover.

'Nothing here is real.' That is Nawab. Back home, he has walked into their conversation.

'The life they promise to the wages they give . . . the swaying palms in malls to the smiles you see on posters . . . all is plastic.'

'Why do you stay then?' asks Ravi.

'Till it suits me, I will,' confesses Nawab. 'The day the dice turns . . . I'll run back.'

'And I was going to hang myself. I can't show Bhaiya my face now, I thought.'

Shivam's taken aback by this statement. Ravi is always strutting around with such swag . . . He could never have dreamed that this guy, when troubled, would give up. So *little, one knows of the world. You think you know people . . . but you don't.*

He scolds Ravi. 'It's your life. Not Shankar Bhaiya's. What that Shankar and his clan think of you is not important. You are a brother, not a cash dispenser . . . stop acting like one.'

'Tomorrow, if you can't take a 46-inch colour TV home, will they not accept you?' Nawab asks. 'And if they don't . . . hang them, not yourself. Get it?'

Nawab has given him clarity. Ravi gets up and hugs him. Shivam's impressed too and joins them for a group hug.

However, he can't sleep that night. His state is worse than Ravi's. The cook could look for another job. But for him, there is just that one girl in this world. And no matter where he goes or how much he tries . . . he is losing. He has just enough for the return ticket home and needs to book it . . . before he runs out of cash. But he can't, knowing she is here . . . he has seen her. He can't leave her and go. He can't. Ever.

After the dust storm of the night, the day dawns bright and sunny. Shivam's mind is in a haze. He does not know where to go next or how.

'Come with me to the mosque,' Nawab invites Ravi. 'Today is an off day for me.'

'You too, designer sahib,' Nawab ambles over to Shivam. *Designer sahib! Who used to call him that? Kitty! Yes, Kitty, in India. A whole world away all of that seems.*

Nawab has made the decision for him. To God's house, go all three. The Jumeirah Mosque is probably the most photographed mosque in the Emirates. Those who come to sightsee it outmatch those who come to pray.

'It's built in the Fatimid style,' the guide is explaining.

Shivam is not interested in the architecture of the place or the ambience of the grounds. All he wants is some peace of mind. And her. Both elude him. Nawab is joking with Ravi and him as they move in tandem with a tourist group that's on a guided tour.

All of a sudden, a stream of schoolchildren floods the place. The place rings with their cries and chatter. The tiny monsters—in sky blue uniform with matching ties—come marching in. Nawab goofs around with a turbaned Indian boy, showing him a trick with his fingers. The boy gives him a toffee in return. He offers one to Ravi too.

'My toffee?' Shivam puts out his hand and asks.

The boy pulls his pockets inside out to show they're empty now. A handkerchief drops out. He offers Shivam that instead. Shivam picks it up to return it to him but the boy runs off. As they enter the mosque to pray, Shivam ties the hanky around his forehead.

It's surreal in there, so many heads bowed together in prayer. To the Almighty, who alone has the power to grant everyone's wishes. Shivam feels empty. *Does he need to pray when God already knows what is in his heart?* Eyes closed, head bowed, he simply surrenders to the power and awaits his destiny.

Flashes of orange suddenly distract him. His eyes snap open. There's a sense of déjà vu. He looks around, frantic. For what . . . he knows not. This cat-and-mouse game is getting too much. All his nerves are frayed. Flustered, he runs out and runs into Nawab, who is putting on his shoes.

'Are you, okay?' he asks.

'It's a mirage I'm chasing,' he cries out, his voice not sounding his own.

'Do you want water?'

Nawab has never seen him in such bad shape.

Shivam sits on a ledge, breathing hard.

'I've been a liar, Nawab,' he says.

Ravi puts a hand on his shoulder.

'You think I'm looking for a job . . . I'm not.'

'Don't panic . . . it's okay,' Nawab reassures him. 'You'll find one.'

'You don't understand.' Shivam's voice gets louder. 'It's her . . . I came for her . . . but it's no use . . . before she appears . . . she disappears. Yes. Just vanishes!'

'What?'

'I'm running after a mirage.' He keeps repeating himself.

Not really getting what he says, Nawab and Ravi ask him to calm down. He is sweating.

'Take that hanky off your head,' Nawab tells him.

Unknotting it, Shivam uses it to wipe his face. He needs some space. His mind is in a whirl. He gets up and walks out, away from the mosque, its tourists and devotees, wanting to forget everything. And everyone. Even the children prancing before him. *Children! It's the same group he has seen earlier. Yes, same sky-blue uniform.* He looks around for the boy whose handkerchief he has. He sees him getting into a school bus and runs to catch up.

And then he freezes. Metres before the bus, he freezes. There she stands, right in front of him, in the bus, helping the last boy board.

It is her. The way she turns, the way she bends and moves and even the way she scratches her nose . . . all of it unchanged. It turns his insides jelly again, just like it did years ago. *It is her.* And her arm, he sees her reach out to pull the boy in, and on it dangles a bracelet, the same charm bracelet, his first and last gift to her.

He calls out, forcing his jammed feet to move. The bus door closes even as he screams out her name.

'Aaina! Wait!'

Sprinting up to the bus, he throws himself against its door, pleading the driver to open up. He bangs on it hard but the bus has started moving. Desperate, he clambers up to the hand safety rail running by the windows of the school bus.

'Aaina . . . Aaina!' He cries out, hanging there.

The bus turns, throwing him off balance. It takes all his strength to hold on. He is crawling up the rail, to the faces crowding the bus window. Kids and more kids . . . screaming, pointing at him . . . in fear . . . and in glee. And then she comes . . . to his window . . . and tries to wrest it open.

The bus brakes. This knocks one of his hands off the rail. He hangs in the air . . . his mind less on the rail and more on the girl reaching out to him at the window. 'Got you . . . '

Then someone knocks him down. He hits the ground hard, on his back. He tries getting up . . . he had to get to her before she disappears again. But there's someone holding him down. Someone in uniform. Two men . . . no, three. And there are more running in. Cops and people are suddenly . . . all over him. It is a high-security religious and tourist site. Even a squirrel bouncing out of line would raise an alarm here. And he was hijacking a bus . . . that's what he overhears someone in the crowd say. Shivam's body sags.

Done. He is done. No way can he get to her now.

'Shivam!' Aaina calls out to him. Stepping off the bus, she runs towards him.

'Shivam!'

He is alive again. Smiling. Smiling in the sun with the tears streaming down his eyes.

Yes, he's found her!

34

A week later, on the bus to Ayodhya

Trees and fields flit by, faster as the bus gathers speed. He has crossed Agra. Kannauj. Next is Lucknow. Once Barabanki passes, Ayodhya's just round the corner. Ten hours, they have said when he started.

Even if it's fifteen, what's the hurry? A whole lifetime he's got. Alone. And empty.

Shivam shuts his eyes. But he can't blot out the world. All of it comes back . . .

Just as she broke free and came dancing back into his life, they handcuffed him. Clasped metal on his wrists. Before he could take her in his arms, they took him into custody. They marched him off, head bent and hands at the back, not even allowing his eyes to have their fill of her, see if she was exactly as he remembered her. They hauled him off in the opposite direction.

He saw Nawab and Ravi on the way, watching him from a safe vantage point in the crowd. Their eyes were large with astonishment and fear. They were too scared to come forward. *It doesn't matter.* His eyes told theirs. *Nothing matters now. All he had was lost. Again.*

She sat on the pavement and cried after they took him away. Thankfully, he had not seen that. Otherwise, he would have been unable to carry the weight of her grief on top of his own.

The Dubai drama ended. First, detention. Then, deportation. They refused his explanation that he came after her.

'On tourist visa, you're only supposed to sightsee. And shop.'

'After years, I have found her,' he said. 'Was just trying to make contact . . . before the bus left.'

'A public nuisance . . . that's what you were making of yourself,' the officer bombarded him. 'And that's a big crime here . . . big penalty.'

His pockets were not big enough to pay up. He had seven days visa left and just enough for the return ticket.

So they let him go, after a beating and a warning. He was to leave immediately.

Through the entire flight, he tried to figure his next step but couldn't. One thing was certain. After landing in Delhi, he could not restart life as if nothing had happened.

'Bhaiya, we can . . . we'll do it together,' Babloo would insist. He knew that.

His friend had a flight to catch two days later—his once-in-a-lifetime opportunity, courtesy of Chaddhaji.

'Hundred more Chaddhajis will come and go, I can't leave you Bhaiya . . . not now.' That was the song the insane fellow would go on singing. And he would ultimately miss his flight. This too Shivam knew. *He can't let him do that. No. Some battles are his alone.* That's why he headed straight for the Anandpur Bus Terminus from the airport, ensuring his phone stayed switched off. And onward to Ayodhya, the place where it had all begun. It made sense to end it there.

The lanes in his hometown were more crammed than before. Newer shops and . . . zanier products had come up. Only the cows, monkeys and monks looked the same. But he didn't dwell on any of it. He went straight to the bathing ghat—the riverbank glittering with temples, tourists, vendors and devotees. Evening aarti was about to begin in some time. People were beginning to gather for it. Soon, it would be a mad rush of humanity, all come to connect with God at the holy hour.

Shivam heads past them all, to the Sarayu. He takes a boat and sails out. The familiar waters . . . the air . . . the smell of all things around fill him with a nostalgia that entering the town after ten years has not dampened. He begins to cry. He puts down the oars, holds his head in his hands, and cries. He had not cried in this way when he lost his father. And mother. And Aaina. All in one evening. But this evening, he lets go. The tears from his eyes become one with the waters of Sarayu. Still weeping, he picks up his bag and unzips it. From within it, he takes out something that travelled to Dubai and back with him. He holds it against his chest one last time, before setting it afloat in the Sarayu.

'Why did you do that?' Someone scolds him, the voice ringing in the stillness of the waters.

Shivam looks up. His eyes can't believe what they see.

'That's my kurti,' she says.

Shivam is in a daze. 'And I?' he asks her. 'Am I yours too?'

'First, get me to your boat. I'll think and tell.'

Shivam smiles. *As bossy as always. Some things never change.*

Aaina is on a boat too, with a boatman. They were sailing behind him silently, unknown to him. He draws near them and helps her climb into his boat.

He savours his dream, not questioning it, scared it might end.

She gets on the boat. *It is real! She is there with him!*

No further thought . . . or words come to him. She has given him a new lease of life.

He hugs her, tightly.

The boat wobbles. They almost lose balance. He lets go of her and holds the oars instead.

'You'll drown me the minute I come!' she pouts and complains.

'If you leave me, I will,' he says.

'I won't,' she promises him.

'Your job in Dubai?'

'I will rule you. That's my job now.'

That settles it. Shivam breathes easy. 'I won't pay you though,' he teases her.

'You'll pay in kind. I'll make sure of that.'

One thing still nags him. 'Aaina . . . your eyes . . . ?'

In Dubai, on the flight, in the bus, he had wondered about the blue eyes that were not blue any more. They were . . . jet black. *Can blue eyes turn black?*

She goes hot in the face and avoids looking at him.

'Aaina?' He repeats himself, unable to understand.

'I used to wear blue contacts earlier . . . simple.'

'What!'

His eyes crinkle with laughter. *Such a con . . . no wonder he got killed.*

'For fun, first,' she admits, twirling a tendril of her hair round and round one finger self-consciously, 'And then, when I saw you buzzing around, I wore them for you.'

Shivam looks scandalized by her confession.

'God! I fell in love with coloured plastic.'

She hits him then, leaning over to punch him good and proper. And the boat almost topples over. In the distance, the chanting of the aarti begins. They see the lights dancing. Lamps in prayer. As the chants fill the air, hands folded, the two thank God, each praying in their own way.

Much later, he remembers to ask her how she found him.

Pat comes her reply: 'Like you found me.'

It takes much cajoling for her to spill the beans. Nawab and Ravi had gone to her when she sat weeping on that Dubai pavement after his arrest. *She wept for him?* He stares, bowled over by this admission. Two days later, his flatmates had informed her that he was getting deported.

'So I took a flight the same day. Came here and waited. As always . . . I reached first.'

'You're faster . . . I know,' he agrees, letting her have the last word. And then there is complete silence between them. All other things can come later. This is their moment to cherish, theirs' alone.